There was no warning.

Nothing to prepare him. Unexpectedly, emotion, a warmth he hadn't known in years, swamped Pete.

Dark eyes stared up at him, and his throat tightened at the look. It was a look of unconditional trust—a look that made him feel as if he were the only person in the world.

Pete stilled and lowered his head to kiss the tiny brow nestled so trustingly against his chest.

He'd thought he'd known exactly what he wanted in life. But, ironically, one unguarded moment—and one little girl—had just changed all that....

Dear Reader,

Welcome to Silhouette **Special Edition** . . . welcome to romance. Each month, Silhouette **Special Edition** publishes six novels with you in mind—stories of love and life, tales that you can identify with—as well as dream about.

April has some wonderful stories for you. Nora Roberts presents her contribution to THAT SPECIAL WOMAN!—our new promotion that salutes women, and the wonderful men that win them. *Falling for Rachel,* the third installment of THOSE WILD UKRAINIANS, is the tale of lady lawyer Rachel Stanislaski's romance with Zackary Muldoon. Yes, he's a trial, but boy is he worth it!

This month also brings *Hardworking Man,* by Gina Ferris. This is the tender story of Jared Walker and Cassie Browning—and continues the series FAMILY FOUND. And not to be missed is Curtiss Ann Matlock's wonderful third book in THE BREEN MEN series. Remember Matt and Jesse? Well, we now have Rory's story in *True Blue Hearts.*

Rounding out this month are books from other favorite authors: Andrea Edwards, Ada Steward and Jennifer Mikels. It's a month full of Springtime joy!

I hope you enjoy this book, and all of the stories to come! Have a wonderful April!

Sincerely,

Tara Gavin
Senior Editor

JENNIFER MIKELS

YOUR CHILD, MY CHILD

SPECIAL EDITION®

Published by Silhouette Books New York
America's Publisher of Contemporary Romance

SILHOUETTE BOOKS
300 East 42nd St., New York, N.Y. 10017

YOUR CHILD, MY CHILD

Books by Jennifer Mikels

Silhouette Special Edition

A Sporting Affair #66
Whirlwind #124
Remember the Daffodils #478
Double Identity #521
Stargazer #574
Freedom's Just Another Word #623
A Real Charmer #694
A Job for Jack #735
Your Child, My Child #807

Silhouette Romance

Lady of the West #462
Maverick #487
Perfect Partners #511
The Bewitching Hour #551

JENNIFER MIKELS

started out an avid fan of historical novels, which eventually led her to contemporary romances, which in turn led her to try her hand at penning her own novels. She quickly found she preferred romance fiction with its happy endings to the technical writing she'd done for a public relations firm. Between writing and raising two boys, the Phoenix-based author has little time left for hobbies, though she does enjoy cross-country skiing and antique shopping with her husband.

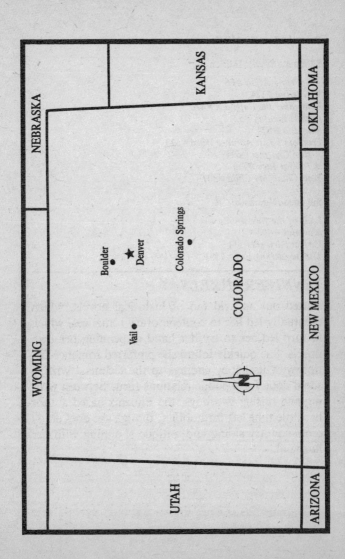

Chapter One

A survivor. Anne recalled that Keith had called her that. Friends claimed she was optimistic and easygoing while the man she'd married had sarcastically described her as a survivor. Well, she was one, she decided, staring out the window at the man walking toward his car. Being victimized in any way didn't sit well with her, nor did crumbling beneath the threats of Keith's father.

Even before the door had closed behind Jerome, she knew she needed distance from him, quiet time to think clearly. She drew a hard breath, trying to calm herself, but her hand shook as she grabbed the telephone receiver and dialed.

Seconds ticked away like an eternity before Karen Winslow said hello.

When Anne finished summarizing her afternoon ordeal, Karen reacted predictably. "I can't believe he came again. What is the matter with him?"

Anne didn't try to explain Jerome Barrett's actions to her friend.

"You can't stay there. He'll drive you crazy. Come to our house."

It was the invitation Anne had hoped for. "It'll only be for a few days..." Her voice trailed off as she heard, in the background, Karen's husband asking about a suitcase for their long-anticipated vacation. How could she have forgotten? Anne wondered. For weeks, Karen had been excited about visiting her mother. "Oh, Karen, I'm sorry. I forgot you were leaving for Florida."

"Don't worry about that. Come, Anne." Karen's voice softened with amusement. "You know Phil hates to leave the house empty. He's afraid someone will steal his baseball-card collection while we're gone. So I'll leave the key with my next-door neighbor, and when we reach my mother's, I'll call you."

Anne unpinned her hair, letting it fall from the sleek chignon she'd worn to work. "Thank you. You're a good friend."

"I'm just sorry that I can't be here for you. But you can hide here as long as you need to."

Anne fought self-pitying thoughts and said a quick goodbye. She didn't want to hide. She simply wanted the nightmare over.

Without giving herself time to relive those moments with Jerome, she punched out her secretary's home phone number. Friends with Anne since she'd begun working for her nine months ago, Linda, too, knew her dilemma.

In her late twenties and a newlywed, Linda had often provided a valuable sympathetic ear when Anne had been distressed. She'd been in Anne's office taking dictation when Anne had received the telephone call that had sent her racing home. "I was worried about you," she said in an almost motherly fashion after their greeting.

For the second time in the past few minutes, Anne capsulized her problem, then offered the assurance, "Everything is all right now, but I'm not coming back into work until Monday."

"Don't worry about anything," Linda said in a cheerful tone meant to ease Anne's concern.

An impossibility, Anne mused. A shipment of holiday apparel was due to arrive. As a department store buyer, Anne's responsibilities weighed heavily on her.

She finished the call, then yanked a suitcase from the shelf above the closet that was filled with sophisticated suits and dramatic dresses. Anne ignored them, and during the next few minutes, she crammed sweatshirts and jeans into the suitcase and tossed toiletries into a bag.

As the wail of a late October wind urged her to dress warmer, she dug into a dresser drawer for a knit cap and scarf. After tucking her hair into the hat, she draped a blue plaid wool scarf around her lower face.

At the door, she paused for a second, and because she didn't know how long she'd be away from home, she tossed several paperbacks into one of the bags.

Ten minutes later, shivering from carting everything to her car, she stomped snow from her boots and reentered the ten-year-old, ranch-style house.

At one time, fine paintings and exquisite furnishings had filled the rooms. She'd had to sell them to pay bills. Possessions meant nothing to her. She'd lived a comfortable life as a child and had never lacked for anything materialistically. What she hadn't had, money couldn't buy.

All her life, she'd searched for love and stability. When she'd married Keith, she'd thought all she'd ever longed for was within reach, but he'd burst that fantasy months after their wedding day.

Another woman might damn the day she'd met a husband who'd offered nothing but some of the most miserable days of her life. But not Anne. She lifted Rachel from her crib. Despite months of unbelievable worries, Anne had received a gift, a precious one—a daughter.

Annoyed at being awakened, Rachel squirmed. Murmuring soothing words, Anne cradled her close then gave her home one last glance before closing the door behind her.

Out of necessity, she spent twenty minutes driving in circles while repeatedly checking her rearview mirror for the private investigator Jerome had hired. When certain she'd lost the blue sedan trailing her, she circled back and headed toward Karen's home.

Beneath a nearly full moon, the upper-scale Denver suburb looked like a winter wonderland. Soft, fluttering snowflakes danced in the air, dusting the ground and the peaks of distant mountains with a fresh carpet of white.

Weariness seeped in as she made the final turn toward the Winslows' home. The phone calls, the packing and the drive had taken longer than she'd expected. Negotiating the car into the driveway, Anne noted that the house to the right of Karen's was dark, but at the living room window of the one to the left, a man peered out as if waiting for someone.

He was tall and fair-haired, and no stranger to her, though she'd never actually met him. Repeatedly while trying to play matchmaker, Karen had raved about her gorgeous bachelor neighbor. Anne hoped he was also congenial about having his doorbell rung at midnight. She had her doubts, as he whipped away from the window in a movement that declared a no-nonsense attitude.

With a casual shrug of her shoulders, she switched off the ignition. Hope for the best, she told herself, unbuckling Rachel from her car seat.

Half-asleep, Rachel bobbed her head to one side and whimpered a protest while Anne bundled her in a blanket. The diaper bag and her shoulder bag slung over her shoulder, Anne snuggled her daughter close to her chest. She closed the car door with one hip and turned around. Head bowed against the onslaught of snowflakes, she plowed forward through a snowdrift.

Nothing was going as planned. The wind whipped at her almost tauntingly while she watched the huge bungalow darken room by room. Even before she reached the front steps of his home, all visible light was gone.

* * *

Pete Hogan downed the last of a cold cup of coffee and entered his bedroom. With his thumb and index finger, he rubbed at the corners of his eyes, blurry from reading thirty pages of a contract about a merger. A conscientious nature compelled him nightly to drag home a briefcase that was fat with stacks of legal papers.

Tired now, he felt like dropping onto the bed. He spent many nights in the same manner. That was all right with him. If his social life was curtailed, it was by choice. For most of his life, success, not love, had been his guiding force.

Yawning, he was unbuckling his belt when the doorbell chimed. For a split second, he considered ignoring it. No friends of his would visit at midnight, but he gave thought to his neighbor two doors away. If Norma Ashby, alone and elderly, had a problem, she would roust him at any time of the night.

Conscience made him pad through the dark house to the front door. He hit the light switch, expecting to see the frail, gray-haired woman and saw no one. On an oath, he flicked off the light and retraced his path toward the bedroom. He was halfway there when garbage cans clattered between the houses.

A youngster's prank? Or a burglar?

Pete didn't think twice. A sensible man showed some caution. Reaching the kitchen, he groped inside the broom closet for a baseball bat. He'd been raised in the inner city; he knew the tricks. Ring the front doorbell while cohorts circle to the back and break in.

Despite a howling wind, he could hear his back porch steps creaking beneath the weight of someone. He gripped the bat tighter, then pressed close to his back door window and squinted into inky darkness.

Enormous dark eyes peered back at him.

He delivered a quick, if internal, "mice or men" lecture, raised the bat and flung open the door. With the flick of the switch, the porch light fell across those eyes.

"Hi." The voice, a smoky, feminine one, came from somewhere between a knitted cap pulled low to her eyebrows and a wool scarf riding high to the bridge of her nose.

"What do you want?"

Anxiously Anne eyed the raised bat. "I'm Anne. Anne LeClare. Karen's friend."

She'd announced her name as if it should ring a bell with him. Though they'd never been introduced, he did know of her. For months, Karen had sung praises about her good friend Anne. Anne made heavenly spinach lasagna. She nurtured plants, loved to swim and played a "mean" game of racquetball. Eyeing the package cradled in her arm, a bundle enveloped in a pale pink quilt, Pete also knew she was a mother, although the specifics about her single state escaped him at the moment.

Softly, even a little nervously, she laughed and tugged down the scarf. "I'm really sorry it's so late," she said. "Karen knew I was coming. I'm supposed to house-sit for them."

Pete raised his gaze from the teddy bear design on the quilt and saw apprehension in the eyes fixed on the bat.

Visibly she shivered. "Could you lower that, please?"

He felt suddenly foolish. No more than five foot four, she was hardly a threat. He noted that the scarf had hidden a knock-out face, delicate and oval-shaped with a small nose and a seductive mouth.

After the Winslows had moved into their home, she'd visited. While washing his car one Saturday afternoon months ago, he'd watched the wind playing with her dark hair as she'd lounged beside the Winslows' swimming pool. He'd heard her laugh, but what he remembered most were the greatest-looking legs he'd ever seen. She looked different now, her cheeks flushed from the cold, her stance tense.

"It's incredibly cold out here." Impatience etched a faint frown line between her dark brows. "I don't mind for myself, but this is terrible weather for Rachel."

He gestured in the direction of her bundle. "Rachel?"

She shifted the baby as if its weight were cramping her arm. "Yes, that's Rachel, my daughter. Could we discuss this inside?"

As the chilly air sliced through him, he saw no point in freezing while they cleared up this misunderstanding. "Come on in." A fragrance that reminded him more of springtime than winter's chill breezed past him.

"If you're concerned that I'm not who I say I am, well, you can ask me anything. I can tell you anything you need to know about the Winslows," she said in one breath. "Probably some things you don't want to know. I used to work with Karen in the lingerie department at Lindsen's Department Store. We've been friends for ages and ages, and Phil owns Phil's Bugs Away. He has a Volkswagen. On top of it is a silly-looking black beetle with yellow polka dots."

Pete grinned slightly at her nervous prattle and the memory she stirred. Some less tolerant neighbors referred to Phil's car with its monstrous replica of a beetle on the roof as "the beast." It had created a ruckus when it first appeared in the neighborhood of expensive cars. "I don't doubt that you know them," he assured her.

She sighed with relief and whipped off the knit cap.

Black hair tumbled around her shoulders, almost inviting his touch. As an unexpected urge to do just that whipped through him, he stepped back. "I still don't understand. What do you want from me?"

"Karen told me that since she and Phil were going to her mother's, I could get the key from you."

"You came to the wrong place. I don't have it," he said more curtly than he'd intended.

A frown deepened a line between her brows. "You don't..." She bit down on her bottom lip in a small show of nerves.

Though he didn't think solving her problem was his business, he offered logical advice. "You could call the Winslows tomorrow morning."

She sent him an exasperated look. "I don't think you understand."

Pete bristled at the way she measured her words as if he were dense. He wanted to assure her that he had an above-average intelligence. As a lawyer, he was trained to listen. He'd heard every word that she'd said.

"Since Karen and Phil are driving across country to her mother's, I can't reach them." For a long moment, she stared at the floor with an expression of disbelief then shook her head slowly. "Wrong house."

He couldn't see what was so traumatic about the mistake. She looked up, pinning him with her dark eyes. Beautiful eyes, Pete noted.

"I noticed the lights were off at the other neighbor's house. Do you think they might be watching television in the dark?"

He smiled at her hopeful tone. "Nope." A tiny hand poked in the air from the folds of the pink quilt, grabbing his attention. Up until now, Pete had forgotten about the baby. "Is there something wrong with it?"

"*It* is a she," she said tightly, making no effort to hide her displeasure.

Pete guessed some of her annoyance with herself was passing onto him. He also sensed by the deadly look fixed on him that he was dangerously close to insulting what was near and dear to her heart, but he knew nothing about babies. "She isn't sick, is she?" he asked as the baby made strange, squeaky sounds.

"There's nothing wrong with her," she informed him.

Pete craned his neck to see the face in the folds of the blanket. "Except she's squealing?"

Anne decided that he knew zilch about babies. "Next week her vocabulary will encompass *Webster's Dictionary*. This week, we get squeals."

Was she laughing at him? He wasn't sure, but neither her feistiness nor her humor slipped past him. A tinge of admiration mingled in with his initial annoyance at being disturbed. Despite her smallness, this woman wasn't prone to knuckling under easily to anyone.

Head bent, her gloved hand curving around her daughter's round underside, she sighed in the manner of someone who believed Murphy's Law had taken over. "She needs to be changed."

Pete dragged his attention away from the snowflake hanging to the tip of a soot-black eyelash. What did she expect *him* to do about that announcement?

She gave him a semblance of a smile. "Obviously the other neighbor has the key, but at the moment, I have an immediate problem. I need to change my daughter. So where—"

This was becoming too complicated to suit him. "You want to change her diaper?" he asked dumbly. While he tried to get a grip on what was happening, she rushed into action, skirted around the kitchen table and headed toward the dining room. Dumbfounded, Pete stared after her. Where in the hell was she going?

Anne had given up waiting for him to play perfect host. Some things required action that surpassed polite pleasantries. In her mind, this was one of those moments. She wasn't going to let Rachel get diaper rash while he made a decision.

She'd scanned his kitchen for a place to change Rachel and had decided against it. It was sterile looking. All white. Too stark for her taste. She liked color. Her own kitchen was filled with vases containing dried baby's breath and mums, a mug collection and a shelf packed with cook books.

His living room offered a similar starkness. There were no plants or animals in his home. The few Japanese sculptures on glass tables emphasized a quiet, ethereal mood. The sleek furnishings were obviously selected for easy maintenance.

In passing, she noted an expensive briefcase and stacks of paper strewn across the top of a polished ebony desk. She pegged him as a workaholic, a man who managed his life on a tight schedule, someone who liked solitude, maybe even cherished it.

With a glance away from his white sectional, she saw his frown and felt like smiling. He appeared truly baffled. "I don't think I should change Rachel on this. Sometimes she's a little messy."

A pained look flickered in his eyes. As if a vivid image had flashed through his mind, he thrust an arm toward his bedroom. "That way."

That way was a hallway that led to a bedroom big enough for two king-size beds. There was only one. Anne noticed a valet in one corner. It held a suit that cost more than she'd made in two weeks when she'd been a salesgirl. Propped against a wall near an ebony dresser were skis. A rowing machine occupied space nearby, and a small portable television on a dresser was blaring away.

Bent over the bed, she unwrapped the last of several blankets wrapped around Rachel. "You're such a good girl." She looked up at the television to see Bacall cozying up to Bogart. "You watch the late-night movies, too?" she asked. Uncannily she'd been aware he was standing near, though she hadn't looked away from Rachel. "I love this one. It's..." She cut her words short as he flicked off the television. Anne sloughed aside his act. Clearly it conveyed that he didn't want an uninvited guest to feel too comfortable. He didn't have to worry. She wasn't too keen on spending too much time with him, either, although he was as great-looking as Karen had claimed.

Rangy-looking because of his height, he had a well-toned body and upper arms that bulged with muscle. Neatly cut blond hair brushed the tips of his ears and fell over the collar of his polo shirt. High cheekbones accentuated a chiseled nose that defied anyone to call him pretty. Determinedly Anne ignored the faint tremor in her own midsection. He also had a slashing, direct stare, an unnerving one that emphasized his unapproachable manner. She wondered what, other than his looks, Karen had found so wonderful about him. "This will only take a minute," she assured him, not doubting that she was infringing on the time he'd designated for sleep.

Wide-eyed, Rachel scanned the strange surroundings. Her small arms and legs thrashing in the air, she babbled as if giving the man standing at the foot of the bed her approval of his home.

Anne smiled at her daughter's friendliness. "She likes you."

Pete wasn't stupid. Who did she think she was kidding? He'd heard friends talk about their babies. The kid had a gas pain.

At the slight quirk of his eyebrow, Anne could see he wasn't impressed. Mentally she shook her head, mystified at why Karen thought he was so great. Never one to give up easily, Anne reminded herself to look for the best in people. Maybe she wasn't trying hard enough to be friendly. "Your name is Pete, isn't it?"

"Pete Hogan," he answered.

From Karen, Anne had received a thumbnail sketch of him. Logically she assumed her friend had given her equal time. "I guess Karen told you about me."

"A little."

His stingy responses nettled her. He could at least make an effort to be friendly. Karen had said he was a good conversationalist. Karen had said a lot more. Anne knew he skied, slept late and chose willowy blondes.

While attempting to convince Anne to accept an introduction to him, Karen had expounded about diversification being good for a person. Anne, a petite brunette, was the answer to Pete's happiness. And of course, Karen was certain that he was the man for Anne. So far, Anne wasn't too impressed with him. "I really appreciate your letting us come in. After all, we are strangers." She tucked little legs and arms back into the pajamas and went on in the same breath. "Here. Would you take this please?"

Disbelief flashed in his eyes as he looked at the soiled diaper she was holding out to him. "Take it? You want me to take it?"

Anne bent her head for a second to veil her grin. "And throw it away." Certain she had control over a laugh, she looked sidelong at him. "Is something wrong?"

There was nothing, absolutely nothing wrong with him, Pete wanted to assure her. He was successful. His friends viewed him as reliable, practical and steadfast. His colleagues described him as a go-getter. He prided himself on controlling all facets of his life. He'd set goals fifteen years ago. At thirty-five, he was close to grabbing the brass ring. But not once during that time had his education included baby care.

"You haven't been around a baby very much, have you?" she asked, still holding out the diaper.

She smiled and something fluttered in Pete's gut. He didn't like it one bit. "Not in a long time. I'm a lawyer, not a pediatrician."

"Still, it's almost impossible that you've never had contact with an infant before."

"By choice," he said firmly.

Her smile waned. "Oh."

"Babies are nice. For other people," he added quickly, regretting his bluntness. As her lips curved to a tolerant grin, Pete searched for a reason that would exonerate him from being tagged hard-hearted. "I'm a bachelor. I have a career."

"Many men are afraid of babies."

Macho pride rose in protest. "I'm not afraid."

Afraid was the wrong word, Anne knew instantly. There was an edge of toughness to him that declared he wouldn't fear very much. What she'd misinterpreted was something else. Maybe dislike. "Well, we need to throw this away," she said, having difficulty believing Karen would try to fix her up with a man who didn't like children.

With reluctance, Pete pinched the diaper with two fingers and held it at arm's length.

Walking toward the kitchen, he wished that he'd told her he wasn't too thrilled with the "we" business.

Ceremoniously he dumped the soiled diaper into the garbage can and slammed the lid; then he ambled back to the bedroom.

No one had ever accused him of being afraid of anything. He'd been raised in a neighborhood where a boy learned early that showing fear made him a victim. He'd lived by his wits, brawling only to prove he wasn't chicken, yet never joining a gang. He'd been as street smart and as tough as friends but wiser. Some of them had been sitting in prison while he'd been working his way through college. It had been his intelligence, not his fists, that had purged him from poverty. If he had ever feared anything, it would have been never getting free of his beginnings.

He stopped in midstride at the bedroom doorway. She'd removed her coat and was fishing in the bottom of a diaper bag. Wispy-looking, almost too thin, she released an exasperated sigh and dumped the contents from the bag.

Through a narrow-eyed stare, he viewed the mess strewn across his white carpeting. "Are you done?"

"Yes, she's sweet-smelling again."

That wasn't what he'd meant. Either she had an IQ equivalent to the freezing temperature outside, or she was being deliberately dense. He decided on the latter.

Perched on the edge of the bed with the baby in her arms, she slipped off her boots. It—she, he mentally corrected—was sucking greedily, her tiny hand clutching the bottle filled with colored water. A sweet, enticing smell clung to the air.

"Poor thing, she was so tired." Lovingly she ran a hand over the top of the baby's head. "Too much late-night traveling."

Pete noticed the baby's eyelids were nearly closed. "Why are you here?"

"I told you. To house-sit."

He looked up from her stockinged toes curling into his carpet and glanced at her bare ring finger. Her answer was too simple, and he wished now he'd paid more attention to Karen when she'd talked about her friend.

"I'm not too sure what to do now." She stared straight ahead instead of at him as if asking the air for advice. "You think it's too late to ring the other neighbor's doorbell?"

Pete supplied a name. "Mrs. Ashby. She believes in strength through rest. Lights are usually out at her house by eight-thirty at night. Why don't you go back home?"

Her brows drew together as if her head was pounding. "Can't. The painters are in. The house smells dreadful."

She kept her head bent. Pete would have liked to see her eyes. Used to observing people for the truth in their words, he'd learned the eyes always betrayed a lie.

As she released what sounded like a small laugh, he saw nothing humorous in her situation. *The Perils of Pauline* came to mind. He visualized her on the street, driving through the snowstorm while he nestled in his warm bed and twitched an imaginary mustache. A desire to stay uninvolved warred with some outdated chivalrous notions that he'd never been able to suppress completely. "I guess you could stay here tonight."

Anne raised her head slowly. The look on his face was almost comical. It wasn't difficult to guess that he already regretted his words, and she couldn't honestly say she felt relief. But his invitation eliminated her taking Rachel out again in a snowstorm. "You wouldn't mind?"

"I'd think you would. You don't know me."

A touch of humor accented her smoky voice. "I'm not worried. Karen has mentioned you often. She said you're the responsible type."

"I bet she did. What color are my socks?" he asked, certain she was as aware of Karen's attempts at playing Cupid as he was.

She smiled then, slowly and a little amused. "She wasn't that detailed." Visually she circled his bedroom. "Two bedrooms or three?"

"Three."

"Could I see one of the other bedrooms? It's way past Rachel's bedtime."

He stared at the baby in her arms, sleeping peacefully. "Stay in here. It'll simplify the moment."

Anne's first impression of him softened. With one thoughtful gesture, he'd belied his unapproachable, intimidating manner. "That's very nice of you." She wrapped Rachel in the blanket again. "If you'll watch the baby..." She didn't bother to finish her request. Visibly he stiffened in the manner of someone just poked in the back.

"I don't baby-sit."

"I wasn't expecting you to," she returned, not deaf to the coolness she'd heard in his voice. "Couldn't you watch her for a minute, though, while I run out to the car for the Portacrib?"

Taking a long breath, Pete tempered the storm he felt brewing in him and snatched his parka from the closet. "I'll get it. Give me the keys."

"The car isn't locked, but you'll need the keys to open the trunk," she said, easing the baby to the bed.

"You didn't lock your car?"

"Shh." She glared back at him. "You'll wake her." She fussed with the collar on her daughter's pink-and-white sleeper. "It's an old car. I even worried that it would break down before I got here. I can't imagine anyone stealing it."

"Birds don't fly, either." Zipping up his jacket, he marched toward the living room sofa and his shoes. She wasn't too sensible. He wiggled his feet, minus socks, into sneakers. She'd driven from somewhere with a child in a car that might break down. She was inside a stranger's home. And she didn't believe in locking her car. Dumb behavior for a beautiful woman.

Letting out a long breath, he stomped out the door. A trek in the cold night air to her car might be exactly what he needed, he decided.

Outside, a chilling wind whipped at the bottom of his jacket. Darkness mantled the Winslows' driveway, but Pete could see Anne's dark-colored car, an eight-year-old compact, rusted around the wheel wells. The back seat was jammed to the headliner with boxes.

He cursed his soft nature that he usually kept repressed and shuffled through the snow. She could stay only for the night. Tomorrow, she had to be gone. He had invited co-workers to a dinner party. What he didn't need was a baby and her strange mother hanging around. Definitely, they'd be gone tomorrow morning.

He opened the trunk, took out and tucked the folded Portacrib under an arm. For good measure, he grabbed the suitcase. He didn't plan to make this trip again because she couldn't do without a hairbrush.

Anne drew a long, deep breath and sank to the mattress. God, how could she have done such a thing to a stranger? She could imagine he thought her the pushiest woman he'd ever met. But she'd had little choice. Where could she have gone with Rachel? To a motel? She'd have been too easy for the private investigator to find.

A bang behind her whipped her to a stand. He shot her another cool, direct look as he struggled with the collapsed Portacrib. A frown marring his brow, he bent over to open one side of the crib.

Anne busied herself with folding Rachel's blanket. She wanted to tell him she was sorry for intruding, for disrupting his life, for bulldozing her way into his home, but for Rachel's sake, she would remain silent. At his lusty oath, she slanted a look back and saw him peering at the side of his finger. "Pinch it?"

"Yeah."

"I should have warned you. Sorry. One side always springs back until the latch is in place."

"Thanks for telling me," he grumbled.

Anne veiled a smile and rounded the bed to open the other side of the crib. "Seems to me it's snowing awfully early this year." When he offered no response, she went on, "It's not even Halloween, and here we are right in the middle of what might be a blizzard. But I always liked winter. Do you?"

"Sometimes," he answered stingily.

"Karen said you don't like to shovel snow. I've always liked to. It's forced quiet time when a person can think out troubles."

"I'll show you where the snow shovel is."

Was that a stab at humor? Anne wondered and released an uncertain laugh. "To pay my way?"

"To work out your troubles. You have them, don't you?"

Too much perceptiveness, she warned herself. Keeping her head bent, she averted her gaze. Since she'd already told one lie tonight about the painters, she'd like to avoid a second one. She was a lousy liar. One look into her eyes, and he'd toss her out, deservedly so. She'd done some silly things in her life. Who hadn't? But barging into the wrong house might rank in the top ten. "Doesn't everyone have some?"

As she dropped to her knees and gathered the contents of the diaper bag, Pete eyed her left hand again. Even if there was no wedding band, the possibility of an abusive ex-husband or boyfriend existed. In his work, he often talked to troubled people. Some were sullen. Others were like her, saying too much, acting too cheerful. He couldn't help wondering what was wrong in her life. Tonight he wouldn't ask. He needed sleep more than he needed answers to questions. "Is she going to be warm enough?" he asked, motioning toward the baby.

"She's wearing a sleeper, and if one blanket isn't enough, I have more."

"Then I'll leave you alone." He snatched up his Scott Turow paperback.

"Do you mind if I hang this on a light fixture?"

Pete paused in midstride.

She was lifting a mobile of several colorful, miniature stuffed elephants out of the diaper bag.

"Then if Rachel wakes up during the night, she'll see something familiar."

With a glance at his wristwatch, Pete silently cursed. It was nearly one o'clock. He had to prepare a brief in the morning. He needed sleep. But if she was right, he sensed that he'd get less sleep when a frightened, crying baby awakened him two hours from now. "I'll get a step stool."

Twice he yawned before returning to the bedroom.

When he set the step stool beneath the light fixture, she moved closer. "I'll hang it."

Pete knew differently but swept a hand toward the stool. While she climbed to the seat, he took a leisurely look at a too-close view of slender legs. The bright orange, knee-length football jersey that she'd changed into rose even more as she stretched. He must be tired, or she wouldn't be tripping the alarm bell within him so easily. He'd seen better. Then reconsidered. Not much better. Before he made a damn fool out of himself, he snatched the mobile dangling from her fingers. "Let me."

As his fingers brushed hers, he felt something stir deep within him. A man comfortable with his own needs, he knew when to back away. At the moment, the smartest thing he could do was get the hell out of the bedroom.

Within seconds, the elephants were dancing happily beneath the light fixture. Pete backed off the step stool, not tempting himself to look at her, and headed for the door. Tired or not, he doubted he'd fall asleep quickly.

At the closing of the door, Anne stood still for a long moment, not certain what she'd felt when their hands had met. With a little shake of her head, she bent over Rachel and tucked another blanket around her. "He isn't pleased to have us." Lightly she smoothed down strands of her daughter's wispy dark hair. "But we had no choice."

Tomorrow, she'd think everything out more clearly. She pulled back the heavy black-and-white comforter and slid under it. Tomorrow, she'd tell him how sorry she was for imposing on him. It wasn't something she'd wanted to do. Pride had warred with her common sense and her thoughts about Rachel. Her child had needed shelter, and for Rachel, Anne would do anything.

Chapter Two

Pete buried his head beneath his pillow to end the nightmare and a screaming banshee's shrilling cry. The wail continued, loud and droning, resounding through the rooms as if someone had parked an ambulance inside his house. With a groan, he squinted at the illuminated hands on his wristwatch. Five-thirty. It couldn't be five-thirty!

Usually his alarm rang at seven-thirty. He never hit the snooze button, but he stayed in bed, stretched and contemplated the business day ahead.

But this wasn't like other mornings, he remembered quickly. He flung his pillow across the room. He'd been generous, hospitable. Hell, he'd offered more than what was required of a good neighbor, but this disruption in his life had to stop. He would inform mother and child that squatter's rights didn't apply in his home, and he wanted them gone within the hour.

Yanking up his jeans, he was convinced that some intangible force was against him this morning. Why else would his quiet, controlled life have changed so drastically in less than twenty-four hours? Now more than ever, he needed to keep a low public profile. Any scandal attached to his name and he could kiss his career goodbye. If for no other reason than protecting his own backside, he needed answers.

The moment he left the bedroom, he smelled the freshly brewed coffee. A chambray shirt dangling from his fingers, Pete reached the kitchen doorway, and all of the fight within him slithered away.

She was dressed in a blue silk robe that stopped above her knees and showed more of a lengthy leg than he needed to see before sunrise. Dancing a little two-step, she patted her daughter soothingly on the back. "Shh. Breakfast will be only a minute." She caroled the promise while eyeing the bottle upright in a pan of water. "Just one more minute." Though she looked exhausted, her voice remained gentle and soothing.

Call it a weakness or a ghost from the past, but he believed in championing the underdog. He believed that there was nothing lower than a person climbing over someone who was already down. No psychic power was needed for him to know that despite her smiles and breeziness, Anne LeClare was in trouble.

As she hustled to the stove, Pete glanced in the direction of the morning siren, tears streaming down her pudgy cheeks. Propped now in an expensive-looking car seat, the baby banged her legs against the pad. Briefly she quieted to chew on her fist, and in fascination, stared at the mouse face on top of a colorful toy clock.

"What are you doing up?" Pete asked.

Startled by his voice, the baby jumped and serenaded them again.

Pete didn't think an apology for scaring her would help. "What is *she* doing up?" he asked low. "It's not even six o'clock yet."

"She can't tell time." Anne shot a look of annoyance back at him. She wished she hadn't. She found herself staring at a broad, masculine chest. Smooth and toned and well muscled. Forearms rippled with muscles, too, and looked stone hard. And there wasn't an ounce of flab at his midsection. He was amazingly fit for a man who sat in an office all day. And disturbingly sexy-looking so early in the morning. She managed to stop staring before he caught her and swung back to the stove. "In a minute..." She snatched a bib from the table. "In a minute everything will be back to normal."

Pete doubted that. He watched her shake watery white drops onto the underside of her wrist, then crossed to the coffeepot. "How can someone so small be so loud?"

"Amazing, isn't it?"

He heard the forced cheerfulness in her voice. Settling against the kitchen counter, he drew a deep breath, not liking himself at the moment. This really wasn't anyone's fault, including the slender woman nearby. Misunderstandings happened. Karen Winslow hadn't given her friend thorough instructions or Anne wouldn't be here now. "Did I say good morning?"

"That's all right."

Pete took a hearty sip of the coffee she'd made. It didn't coat his tongue, and the caffeine helped. The baby's cry no longer sounded to him like an imitation of someone's nails clawing a chalkboard. "No, it isn't. I could be civil. I'm not used to waking so abruptly."

Anne had planned to say as little as possible to him, but he was offering a token of friendliness. She never turned her nose up to that. "And you're not used to giving up the comfort of your own bed. You've been a good sport, Mr. —"

Pete paused her with a halting hand. "We're past that. Pete," he insisted. He noticed she hadn't taken time to put on shoes or pour herself a cup of coffee.

"These early mornings are something you have to get used to."

Pete detected a trace of sympathy in her voice and felt worse. "I usually wake up slowly." He could have told her that he'd spent years waking before sunrise to deliver morning newspapers, to work half a day before heading to college and later, to outshine other associates at the law firm. After living for years on only six hours' sleep a night, he felt that he'd paid his dues; he deserved leisurely wake-ups.

Anne looked away from the cereal in the saucepan, grateful to see that he was finally slipping on his shirt. "Rude awakenings are something I'm accustomed to."

Head bent, buttoning his shirt, he moved toward the refrigerator.

The bottle in her hand, she pivoted toward Rachel.

As she took a step to the right, Pete took one to the left to give her room, but the aisle wasn't wide enough.

Against him, he felt the softness of her breast, the sharp point of her hip. Pete shifted sideways to let her pass, but he knew the damage had been done. They'd stood too close for strangers. And for a second too long.

Like it or not, he knew he wasn't immune to a delicate brunette with eyes that a man could drown in. Pouring himself a glass of orange juice, he decided it was good this woman would breeze out of his life as quickly as she'd whisked into it.

Determined to give him a wide berth, Anne glued her backside to the chair in front of Rachel. She'd felt the jolt, the rush of pleasure, but she'd already made excuses for it. It was because it had been so long since she'd stood that close to a man. It had nothing to do with him. "As soon as I've fed Rachel, I'll check with Mrs.—" She paused and waited for him to supply a name again.

"Mrs. Ashby. Norma Ashby," he said, reaching for the orange juice glass. "She's an elderly woman who baby-sits for the Winslows."

"I'll check with her."

Pete understood about chemistry. At some point since she'd entered his home, sparks had been stroked more than once. Regardless of what his brain told him, his body was receiving a different message about her. She looked delicate, almost breakable, the kind of woman that aroused protective instincts in any man.

"Why don't you tell me now why you really didn't want to go home last night?"

Anne shifted on her chair. She'd never doubted that he would ask questions. Intelligence dominated his eyes and had warned her that he would see through her breezy reason for being at Karen's. Still, she didn't know him, didn't trust him enough to confide in him. "I told you." She met his gaze and swore softly under her breath as her pulse jumped. "Painters."

Pete didn't buy the reason this morning any more than he had last night. If he was smart, he wouldn't ask too much, wouldn't get involved in a domestic dispute. He'd already noticed that someone had bought a blue bib for the baby; someone had anticipated a boy. More than once, she'd nervously glanced toward the bay window as if she were waiting for someone. Or hiding from someone.

"Nothing is as complicated as you're imagining," she said with a feigned lightness he didn't believe.

He couldn't stop himself from asking, "Is the baby's father after you?"

She kept her eyes glued on the baby. "You're a man who likes answers, aren't you?"

"Last night we were both tired. Where is he?"

"He died."

Too calmly, too matter-of-factly, too emotionlessly, Pete thought. The baby wasn't six months old, yet Anne's voice was free of grief. "That must have been difficult for you," he said, not knowing what approach to take.

"Losing her would be."

"Losing?"

She slanted a look at him, saw he appeared even more puzzled. "I know that Rachel and I have been disruptive."

And unsettling, Pete mused. He'd thought her divorced or separated but not widowed. She came across as unfeeling about the death of her husband, yet she bubbled with affectionate warmth for her child. She acted wary, but his assumption about her hiding from the baby's father had been wrong. And though a trace of sadness clouded her dark brown eyes, she clung to a positive upbeat mood.

As the bottle squeaked and signaled empty, Pete watched in amazement at the change in her daughter. Grinning, she squealed at her mother. Ridiculous, yes, but Pete felt like an intruder in his own kitchen. A man prone to rationalizing, he assumed what he felt strange about was being in the midst of such a domestic scene. Harder than necessary, he set his cup in the sink.

At the clink against porcelain, the baby tilted her head back and studied him.

Pete smiled tentatively at her, but her dark eyes remained solemn. She was as unnerving as her mother but in a different way. Narrowing his eyes, he delivered his best I-mean-business look. She yawned as if bored. Fortunately he didn't elicit the same response from clients.

Possibly because she looked so harmless, he dropped his guard and stepped closer. It wasn't a wise thing to do.

Her inquiring eyes widened, and as if he'd pinched her, her face squinched and her mouth flew wide with a wail that pierced the air.

Her mother whirled away from the sink with a look of alarm.

Pete raised his hands in the air. "I didn't do anything." He caught the hint of amusement in her eyes. She must have thought him an imbecile with children.

No more Mr. Nice Guy, he told himself, storming toward the sanctuary of the shower. Not too quietly he shut the bedroom door, then stripped to his Jockey shorts and stepped into the bathroom. Something wet and soft squished beneath his foot. Cautiously Pete lifted his foot and stared at a chartreuse-colored sponge shaped like a rhinoceros.

This, he thought, snatching up the sponge and tossing it into the bathroom sink, didn't belong in his house any more than they did. But he'd cope. He was good at coping. All his life he'd coped with less, had made due, had done whatever was necessary to get along. He would handle this unexpected problem, too.

He'd dress and leave. At the office, his life wouldn't seem so chaotic. And this evening when he came home, they'd be gone. For more reasons than the obvious one, that was for the best. He rarely fooled himself and didn't plan to start now. Repeatedly she'd clicked something on inside him, something that he worried he might not be able to turn off if he spent more time with her.

Twenty minutes later, shaved and showered, he ambled to the closet and the rack of suits. There had been a time when he'd lived in a world of graffiti-marked buildings, when he'd owned a pair of scuffed sneakers and worn jeans with holes in the knees. It had been a time when his only possession had been a deflated football that he'd patched.

A lot of years and hard work had helped him escape that life. Gone were the days of playing in a vacant lot, of falling asleep hungry, but the fear of losing all he'd gained never vanished. People claimed he was driven, obsessive about his career. They weren't wrong. He'd been single-minded with one goal in his life and no distractions except the ones he'd allowed. For years, he'd followed his plans—plans he wouldn't change for anyone.

His briefcase in hand, he stepped into the hall. Rock music blared from the kitchen radio. Though a man with an eclectic appreciation for music, he truly hated squealing guitars.

When he entered the kitchen, Anne pivoted away from the bay window and flicked off the radio. She felt uneasy, even a little panicky and couldn't pinpoint why she was letting one man unravel her so. Skimming his expensive dark suit, she knew that instead of thinking about him as a man she should be viewing him as a lawyer. He could provide the advice she needed. He certainly emanated power and confidence, the kind that influenced people. Though his hair was a touch too long in back for the corporate image, it didn't distract. Instead, it lent a rebellious edge to his intimidating looks. A person might wonder about who this man really was and think twice about meeting him head-on. That was exactly the kind of man she might need to go one-on-one with Jerome. "Where do you practice law?"

Placing his briefcase on the table, he looked away and draped his overcoat over the back of a chair. "Klein, Bingington and Reed."

"Impressive."

Pete thought so. Fresh out of law school, he'd been eager to work for them, to be one of their hundred lawyers. Years of hard work passed before they'd noticed him. He never regretted hard work if it brought results. It had. He was close to being offered a partnership.

"Is that a corporate firm?" she asked while nearby her daughter gnawed on a round rubber ring.

"It handles civil cases, too." He slipped on his coat and mentally geared himself for traffic snarled by snow. "I'll be leaving now. If you're hungry, feel free to eat whatever you find. Except the caviar. It's for tonight."

She pulled a face. "I wouldn't think of eating fish eggs for breakfast. You're having a party this evening?"

"People I work with will be over."

"People from the law firm?" She rolled her eyes. "Brilliant deduction." Embarrassed, she fixed a stare on her child's face.

Pete thought her reaction endearing, even a touch innocent. The thought amused him. Anne LeClare looked closer to thirty than her teens and obviously had left innocence behind her when she'd conceived her child. Still, he saw something sweet and innocent in her delicate features.

"I'm surprised you're a corporate lawyer. You don't look as if you'd fit into the button-down world. You look more like a maverick lawyer at the public defender's office.''

His lips stretched to a slow smile. She was amazingly on target. No one ever took him for an Ivy Leaguer. Too many rough edges of his youth still showed. "What do you do?"

"Not what was expected." She smiled with a memory. "All through my childhood I was a tomboy, much to the dismay of my mother. So what do I end up doing for a living," she said rather than asked. "I buy designer fashions." At his puzzled frown, she added, "I'm a buyer for a department store franchise—Lindsen's."

"Like it?"

Running a washcloth under the spigot, she grinned back at him. "Love it."

"That's more important than anything else."

"Well, it's like icing on the cake," Anne answered. She viewed their different outlooks as one of many differences between them. He'd seek goals with success in mind while she'd go after them to give Rachel everything. "I'm sorry Rachel woke you this morning."

Pete could have told her that he didn't have anything against babies. If he acted unfriendly it was because he treasured his privacy, but he saw no point in explaining himself. Without forethought, he scribbled on the notepad by the telephone. "This is my office phone number." He tore off the sheet and set it on the table. "If you need . . ." Pete cut his own words short. What was he going to say? If she needed him?

Of course, she didn't need him. Neither of them did, he reminded himself, with a glance at the baby.

This time she giggled at him. Sparkling dark eyes twinkled above a turned-up nose. He studied her, seeing her mother's delicate features. Her silky-looking dark hair was like Anne's, too. Pete stepped closer, preparing for another scream. Instead, the baby mumbled some gibberish.

He'd never understood what was so grand about kids or about being a family man. His own father had felt nothing but burdened by three sons. Pete didn't plan to fall into the same trap. After years of struggling, he believed the only thing that truly mattered was a man's work.

He shoved back his shirt cuff and glanced at his watch. He had a few more minutes. Challenged by his earlier encounter with the baby, he squatted before her. Sticky fingers probed his lips then grabbed at his nose. He stared into her innocent, dark eyes and lightly brushed a knuckle across her cheek. It was softer than velvet.

Looking over her shoulder, Anne felt her opinion of him gentling. There was a softer side to this man with the curt responses and intimidating stare. She wondered why he worked so hard to stifle it. "I told you she liked you."

He snapped to his feet and set his jaw. He wasn't certain what annoyed him more: the softening sensation he'd felt when touching the baby, her mother catching him at it or the damn tug on his insides now as she smiled at him.

It warmed him. Hell, what didn't? An insidious attraction existed, he realized, as he felt a definite stirring of his blood for a woman who'd offered little encouragement. She had a smoky sound that curled around him, lured him, made him wonder if it would sound the same when breathless during lovemaking. And she had eyes that made him think of a summer's night—and hot sultry air.

"Pete?"

He gave a start. On the wall beside him, the phone was ringing, and by her puzzled frown, he guessed it wasn't the first ring. Annoyed with himself, he yanked the telephone receiver from the hook and barked a hello.

"You don't sound fit for the day ahead of you," Tim Anderson gibed. "I'm calling to remind you that we have that morning meeting."

Behind Pete, the baby warbled a protest at having her fingers wiped. Wincing, he cupped a palm over the receiver to block out Rachel's wail.

Tim's voice perked up predictably. "What was that?"

Pete played dumb. "What was what?"

"That noise."

"Static."

"Bull." Tim laughed. "Hogan, that was a baby."

"That's what it sounded like to me, too."

"What did you do?" Tim went on in an amused tone. "Rent a family?"

Pete leaned a hip against the kitchen counter and released a strained laugh. What if all of this was penance, punishment for being too confident that he determined his own fate?

"Are you finally taking the need for a family image seriously?"

"We'll talk about this when I get to work."

"I won't let you off the hook. I want to know who's there with you." A trace of amusement continued to edge Tim's voice. "Ah, how true some clichés are."

He strained to hear Tim. "What the hell are you talking about?"

"Still waters run deep."

Pete prepared himself for a lengthy explanation when he arrived at the office. And what would he say? Some woman with knock-out good looks needed a place to stay for the night for herself and her baby so he invited them in? The truth sounded unbelievable even to his own ears.

Anne sent him an apologetic grin as he set down the receiver. "She's usually not so cranky, but she's off schedule."

Who wasn't? he thought. He shrugged as if there were no problem and retrieved from the floor a rattle the baby had flung aside.

The irritation was back on his face again, Anne noted. She rocked and patted Rachel. "I promise that we'll be gone when you come home," she said, certain she and her daughter were the reason for the return of his foul mood.

Pete paused at the door and looked back at the chaos in what used to be his neat kitchen. Silently he laughed. He supposed it served him right, pulled him down a peg. Somehow, Anne LeClare and her daughter had forced him to remember that he couldn't control everything in his life.

From one point of the bay window, Anne could see a portion of the street. She listened to the sound of Pete's car engine, then sunk her hands into sudsy dishwater. What a morning. More than once when she'd been feeding Rachel, she'd felt his stare, had been unable to ignore it. She could think of no reason except that he'd incited something within her she'd thought she would never feel again. Something she wanted to resist.

She wanted no involvement with anyone. If she had, it wouldn't be with him. Already she'd noticed too many differences for compatibility. He was a private man; she thrived on the company of friends. He was a slow morning person; she bounded from bed at the ring of the alarm clock. Dozens of differences, she reconfirmed.

Behind her, Rachel squealed gleefully, fascinated by the toy clock. She was so innocent, so unaware.

"You're such a good girl." Anne tucked Rachel's rattle into the oversize diaper bag. She would wait another hour before ringing the doorbell of Karen's other neighbor. If, like Pete, the woman didn't have the key, Anne wasn't certain what she would do.

Despite Pete's charity, she was on her own. That didn't scare her; she'd been on her own a long time, even before her marriage had ended.

Keith had been a weak man, dependent on everything: her, his father and alcohol. He'd taught her a valuable lesson. Love was for other women, not her.

"Bath time," she sang out to Rachel, trying to lift her own spirits.

Rachel answered her with an infectious giggle.

"Everything is going to be all right," Anne whispered, and kissed her daughter's nose. "We're going to—"

She cut her words short, riveting a stare on the back door as someone knocked. Frightening thoughts leapt into her mind. What if she'd been followed? What if she hadn't lost Jerome's private investigator? What if he'd parked his blue sedan on the street in front of Pete's house, just waiting until he left?

All she'd wanted was some peace for a little while, some time to make plans.

Someone rapped harder.

Her pulse pounding, Anne inched closer to the window and peeked through the slats of the venetian blind.

Chapter Three

A small wiry woman with curly gray hair protectively gathered her long cardigan tighter.

Anne opened the door, deciding if she wasn't careful, she'd jump at her own shadow.

A network of lines deepened in the woman's face. "Where's Pete?"

"He's not home."

"Dang, I missed him again. Give him this." She shoved a cellophane-wrapped plate of cookies at Anne. "He loves my chocolate-chip cookies. And I wanted to thank him for shoveling the snow in front of my house."

Anne took the plate and made a hopeful guess. "You're a neighbor. Mrs. Ashby?"

A smile crinkled her face. "Pete's told you about me?"

"Well, not exactly, but you're just the person I wanted to talk to."

"Me?" The woman's breath steamed the air. "I can't imagine what Pete's woman would want with me?"

Pete's woman! "No, wait. You don't understand."

The woman's pale blue eyes swept over her. "You've never visited Pete before. I watch, you know. I'm a good neighbor. I know who comes and goes."

"Forget Pete."

Behind Anne, Rachel gurgled, snagging the woman's attention.

Mrs. Ashby tipped her head to peer around Anne and arched a gray brow. "If you say so."

Anne fought exasperation. She didn't want to alienate this woman or she would never get the key. "Please, listen." Anne managed a pleasant smile. "I'm a friend of Karen's—Karen Winslow." Anne breezed through the details of her arrangement with Karen. To her relief, Norma Ashby smiled.

"Well, why didn't you say so? I have the key."

Relieved, Anne felt her optimism returning. "Let me clean up here first. Then I'll come over and get it from you."

Norma patted her arm. "You do that. I'll make some tea, and you can tell me how long you've been seeing Pete."

"No, I'm not..." Anne was treated to Norma Ashby's squinty glare and dismissed any thought of correcting the woman's misconception. "Yes, we'll talk then."

She shut the door and laughed at Rachel peeking at her through a huge round ring. "We are in for an unusual morning.

"Pete wondered if he'd have to give up his immortal soul. When a man was close to getting everything he'd dreamed of, didn't he always have to pay a price? Was it enough that he'd worked hard toward such a moment as this?

He tuned in Amos Klein again and listened to the names of the two other lawyers being considered for the partnership—Frank Owens and Martin Randall.

One of them would grab the brass ring and become a partner. Klein, Bingington, Reed and Hogan sounded good to Pete. But both of the other men were married, a plus with Klein. Frank could even supply a family of two and a half children. Martin wasn't quite so secure. He'd been married two years and had a daughter, but around the office, gossipmongers still tagged him with the moniker, Roving Randy.

Across the high-gloss conference table, looking pleased with himself, Tim smirked at Pete. His gray eyes gleamed with satisfaction before he lowered his head, offering Pete a view of his receding hairline. Two nights ago over beer and chicken wings, Tim had made a gentleman's wager that Pete would be one of the members considered for the partnership. Glad you won, buddy, Pete mused.

An hour later, shirtsleeves rolled up, Pete caught up with Tim in the reception room that led toward their offices.

Beams from the overhead lighting shone on the plush gray carpet and rosewood desks. The receptionists were immaculate, coiffured and manicured. Silk rustled as one, a tall brunette named Janet, rounded her desk, then paused to smile at Klein.

Behind her desk, the other receptionist pleasantly chanted in a Southern drawl, "Klein, Bingington and Reed."

Feet ahead of Pete, the law firm's senior partner blocked a clear path down the hallway. Nearly seventy, Amos Klein was a distinguished-looking man, tall and lean in his Brooks Brothers suit. Short white hair accentuated the brightness of the shrewd blue eyes watching as Frank Owens rushed up to him.

Yesterday, Klein had entered Pete's office and had pretended casual interest in Pete's personal life. Pete hadn't known his hidden agenda then. With the announcement about the partnership, he was aware he'd be in a fishbowl professionally and personally. Discreetly, Klein would begin digging into the private lives of all three men.

In passing, Pete heard Frank's comment. "My Kathy and I always tell our two kids how important loyalty is."

Tim snorted when they were out of Klein's hearing range. "Frank had to remind Klein that he has a wife and kiddies."

"It's the right image."

"You need to enter the marriage market, too." Tim snagged his arm, determined to grab Pete's full attention. "You've dated the wrong kind of women. High-powered, career-minded types place marriage at the end of a priority list.''

Pete could have told him differently. He'd dated the right type of woman for him, someone interested in her career, not marriage or children.

Over Tim's shoulder, Pete watched Martin Randall, a friendlier competitor for the partnership than Frank, sidling up close to the receptionist. Too close for a married man. "What do you mean?" Pete asked as Janet's hand fluttered to Martin's and squeezed meaningfully.

"I was thinking about the baby's mother."

Pete groaned mentally and resumed walking. Why did he think Tim would forget Rachel's wail? "I don't even know her."

Tim sent him a you're-kidding look. "You must have known her well enough."

"The baby isn't mine." Pete lowered his voice and explained last night's dilemma.

Tim chuckled. "Is she married?"

"Not anymore. She's a widow."

"That's good."

"What's good? That the woman lost her husband?"

Tim grimaced. "No, not that. But you know Klein frowns on divorce."

"Back up. I'm not getting involved with this woman."

"If you did, her status is one that Klein would view as acceptable."

Pete shook his head. "Forget it. She and her child will be gone when I get home."

"Too bad." Amusement edged Tim's voice. "A ready-made family would soar you to the top of the list."

"It's a lousy reason for getting married," Pete countered. Honestly, he couldn't think of a good reason.

Anne readjusted a squirming Rachel and rapped on Mrs. Ashby's door.

It squeaked open a few inches before the woman's pale eyes peered at her. A second passed while she rattled the chain and swung open the door.

At her beckoning, Anne took a step forward. Everything was vintage 1930s from the mahogany furniture and lace doilies to the book on the coffee table, a worn version of *Gone With The Wind.*

"I've made tea." The woman's voice sang out an instant before she sailed away from Anne. "Did Pete mention poor Lolita?" she called back.

Anne shifted Rachel and followed. "Lolita? No, he never mentioned anyone by that name."

"Oh, dear, well he must be working on the case. He promised. If he makes a promise, he keeps it," she said with certainty.

"What is the case about?" Anne asked, trailing the woman into the kitchen.

"Oh, my sister is fighting to keep her cats."

Anne had expected to hear something about securities, fraud or taxes. "Why would someone want to take them from her?"

"Because she's old and a widow and hasn't much money. Such craziness. Criminals run free, and they go after her."

Something wasn't clear to Anne. "Mrs. Ashby, who doesn't want her to keep her cats?"

"The city. They say her animals are a health menace. She lives out in the boonies and has plenty of room. Her second husband had a small ranch," she added. "And she only has about ten dogs and about thirty—no, forty cats. Myrtle, Lolita's tabby, just had eight kittens."

A small cocker pounced toward Anne to be petted. Anne squatted down and brought Rachel's tiny hand across the dog's silky fur. "And Pete is handling her case?"

"Well, he needed to be persuaded. That's Sporty," she said with a grin at the dog. "One of Lolita's finds. When I assured Pete that Lolita's animals weren't a health menace, he agreed to see what he could do."

One thing still didn't make sense to Anne. "If this Mrs.—Lolita—hasn't a lot of money, how is she paying Pete?"

"She isn't paying." Pouring tea into cups, she slanted a curious look at Anne. "You really don't know Pete very well, do you?"

Anne didn't need to be a mind reader to know the woman was wondering if Pete was Rachel's father.

"Let me tell you, it's not surprising that Pete is helping Lolita. Pete knew Lolita from the old neighborhood."

Anne gave her an expectant look. "Where is that?"

The woman rattled an address that fell under the term "the wrong side of the tracks."

It was another revelation that contradicted Anne's first impression of Pete Hogan. She'd thought he'd been born with the proverbial silver spoon in his mouth.

"Sit, sit," Norma commanded while placing cups on the table.

Anne stopped scratching behind the spaniel's ear and dropped to the closest chair, settling Rachel on a thigh. "Do you have any children?"

Norma snorted. "Ever hear of the old woman in the shoe? Nine children and twenty-five grandchildren. If you ever need someone to watch that sweet one," she said with a nod toward Rachel, "you just call me."

Anne felt herself relaxing with the grandmotherly woman and she drank her tea. For months, she'd worried that any stranger might be a spy for Jerome.

Norma hunched forward as Anne set down her nearly empty cup. "Tea leaves tell so much." She squinted at the bottom of the teacup. "Yours has to do with your child and the baby's father."

The reminder about Keith tensed her. It wasn't that she still grieved for him, but so much of what was happening in her life revolved around her daughter being a Barrett.

"He will get all that he longs for," Norma concluded.

Anne wanted to stop the woman's silly game. "That's impossible," she responded as calmly as possible.

"I see what I see," Norma returned in a gruff manner. "Pete will get all that he wants."

Anne mentally berated herself for briefly falling under the woman's fantasy. Standing, she held her palm up for the key. "Pete's not the father," Anne said firmly to set her straight.

Norma merely smiled back at her.

Throughout the day, Pete made slow progress on the provisions of a merger. He swiveled his wing-armed chair away from his desk and stretched to flick off the CD player on the credenza and end Beethoven's Fifth Symphony in midcrescendo. While he enjoyed classical music, he listened to country and western at home, but such selections wafting from his office into the hallways of the staid law firm weren't in his best interest.

Uncharacteristically he whiled away more time. Out his office window, low-hanging clouds blocked the view of skyscrapers. Pete stared with unseeing eyes at them. Before him, an image flashed of a woman with glossy raven hair and eyes so dark, they reminded him of a midnight sky.

In disbelief, he cursed himself and jerked his chair around toward his desk. What the hell was he doing, wasting time thinking about her? Maybe he'd awakened too abruptly this morning. That's what was wrong. What else would account for his daydreaming? Certainly he knew better. Professionally he was where he wanted to be because he hadn't allowed such distractions.

* * *

Half an hour later, snow swirling around him, he climbed the slick steps to his front door. During the drive home, he'd offered himself more reassurances and a warning. Stay away from her.

With only a few hours to shovel the sidewalk and clean the house before company arrived, he rushed into the house and tossed on a gray sweatshirt, jeans and sneakers. He spent the next hour scooting the vacuum around the house, and generally sprucing things up. Then he set the table.

Outside, snow collected on the ground, taunting him. He slipped on his parka, but as he stepped outside, he saw the light from the Winslows' kitchen window. Grumbling to himself about moments of idiocy, he tossed the snow shovel into a snow heap then trudged across the icy walkway between his and his neighbor's home. Old habits died hard, he excused. Because he'd spent too many years looking after his brothers, he felt compelled to play good neighbor Sam. He'd check on her and then forget her.

Through the Winslows' back-door window, he watched her run a hand across tense neck muscles. With her hair secured back with a gold clip, she was dressed in jeans and a turtleneck plus a heavy, green ski sweater and a fleece-lined vest.

He rapped once, then stepped in. He wished he'd waited. She jerked away from the stove with a look garnered by most of the frightened heroines in horror movies. "Hey, I'm sorry."

Anne managed a smile while her heart thudded against the wall of her chest. "This is a surprise."

He could have told her he was just as astonished to be there.

Nerves tight, she didn't feel relief that it was him and not Jerome. "Did I forget something at your place?"

"No. I stopped by for a moment to see if you're settled in."

"Sort of." She sounded nervous, felt nervous. It was ridiculous, but except for a passing wave, she hadn't expected more contact with him. "Want a cup of coffee?"

The strain in her voice held him still. More was wrong. Pete sensed it, saw it in her troubled frown. One cup wouldn't hurt before he picked up the snow shovel. Nodding, he slipped out of his jacket. The smell of bacon hung in air that seemed cool. No, the room was downright close to freezing he realized as a chill raced through him. "Why is it so cold in here?"

She gave him a grin that held no humor. "The furnace conked out about an hour after I lugged everything in. I tried to fix it. Hank was always having to fix the furnace. I thought I'd watched him enough but—" She stopped and held her hands out.

"Who's Hank? A brother?"

"He was the maintenance man at one of the apartment buildings my family lived at. I guess I didn't watch him as carefully as I should have."

Pete couldn't stop a smile from forming. She looked so perplexed that a furnace had gotten the best of her.

"Anyway, it's a hopeless cause."

The steaming brew she'd set on the table invited him to sit back, relax and enjoy the coffee, but a glance at the baby wrapped for subzero temperatures weighed on his conscience. "I'll check."

"Really, you don't have to. I change flat tires and replace electric plugs," she said to his back. "I know when a furnace is a thing of the past."

He was already opening the basement door.

Just as she'd said, the furnace was useless he concluded after checking it out. Pete chanted a few obscenities at it in vain then climbed the stairs. "It's dead," he announced.

She had the good grace not to send him an I-told-you-so look.

"I'd suggest calling a repairman, but you'll never get one at this time of the evening. And I'm not sure Phil and Karen would want you to have it repaired. Phil's been talking about a new one."

Snatching up a dish towel, Anne swung away toward the sink. "As much as I'd hoped for an easy solution, I didn't expect one," she said, grabbing the frying pan from the drainboard.

"You know you can't stay here, don't you?"

He'd said out loud what Anne had been trying to avoid thinking about. She was back to square one with no choice except to return home.

Pete curled fingers around the warm cup of coffee. On the table was a notepad with a long list. He expected a shopping list. Instead of groceries, she'd jotted down things to do: call Karen, pick up work at office, call Michael, stop at cleaners, write Pete a thank-you note. He looked away before she saw him reading it, but he wondered who Michael was.

"Did you see the cookies Mrs. Ashby brought over for you?" she asked, to mask her own worry.

Though puzzled at the shift in conversation, Pete went along with it for the moment. "Best ones in the city."

"It was nice of you to shovel her snow."

"No one has any secrets," he said self-depreciatingly. *Except you.* With a step closer, he tried to see her face. Though he didn't know what was wrong, he wanted to assure her everything would get better. He'd been through hard times, too. The sky only *seemed* to be falling. "Why don't you call the painters and stop the job for a while?"

Anne swung around. "The paint—"

Her eyes gave her away. He could almost hear her calling herself every name for stupid that she could think of. "There aren't any painters, are there?" He didn't wait for her response. "Tell me what's wrong." he insisted. If she told him, maybe he could walk away. Maybe then, whatever fascination he felt for this woman would disappear.

Anne resisted an urge to confide in him. "It's better if I don't."

A smart man would leave it at that. For years, Pete had kept himself free of others' problems. A decade had passed since he'd worried about the well-being of someone other than himself. But as her shoulders straightened, he sensed her fighting spirit and admired her for it. More than anything he appreciated such strength. "I'm a lawyer. We're used to opposition," he reminded her.

She attempted a soft laugh. "It's nothing criminal, but I do have a formidable adversary."

"Who?"

For a long moment, she stared thoughtfully at him as if she were weighing whether or not to trust him. "My father-in-law."

Pete remained silent, waiting.

Almost nervously she ran a hand down her denim thigh. "He wants his granddaughter," she said softly, seeming afraid to say it out loud. "He's been harassing me."

Pete sensed the difficulty she was having. Talking about a problem meant dealing with it on a different level.

"He even has a private investigator following me so he always knows where Rachel is. I can't go home. I needed time away, some quiet time, and Karen offered to let me stay here."

Pete made a guess at the rest of her problem. "And you're afraid he'll find you if you stay at a motel?"

"I'm sure that he already has his man checking them."

How could she have no one to turn to? "What about your family?"

She wagged her head. "My mother died years ago. There isn't anyone anymore."

Unknowingly she'd just reeled him in. He understood her loss. And he understood why this woman who seemed so strong might be even more vulnerable.

"That's not really true, is it? I have a daughter."

Pete heard such pride and affection in her voice that he felt envy. It was an odd emotion for him, one he hadn't felt since he was ten years old, since he'd sat alone with two kid brothers on a Christmas morning and watched them cry because Santa hadn't come. "What about other friends?"

"He knows them all." She sighed in frustration. "I've tried to avoid the police, but—"

Pete shook his head. "Without proof that he made a threat, they can't help you." But *he* could, he thought, with a glance toward the baby. Gleefully she banged a toy against the arm of the car seat. At the moment, he was definitely the one person who could make the child's mother's life easier. "Well, you can't stay here tonight." He drained the coffee in his cup. "Come on."

Anne couldn't hide her surprise. "You don't look like the glutton for punishment type. Have you forgotten this morning's abrupt awakening? And you're having company," she added.

Briefly he wondered for whom she'd spieled off the reasons, him or herself. With a step closer, he caught her arm, halting her from drying a plate.

Anne drew a hard breath. A longing rose within her so quickly, she nearly rocked with it. Ages seemed to have passed since she'd allowed a man's hand to touch her beyond a safe distance. She didn't remember it feeling like this. "I couldn't do that to you again." Somehow she managed to sound steady. "Rachel wakes early, remember?"

"I remember, but you can't stay here," he answered simply, not wanting to analyze his motives too much. "It isn't good for her health."

He hit the right button, a reminder about Rachel's welfare. Anne knew he was right; it was too cold in the house. And she couldn't go home. She thought of a dozen friends who'd open their homes to her. She'd never lost contact with college roommates who'd shared their bags of potato chips and their granola bars while cramming for finals. A few co-workers were bridesmaids at her wedding. But as she'd told Pete, Jerome knew all of her friends. A stranger's home offered the safe haven she needed for her daughter. "I'll get a few of her things together. Then I'll be over."

"I'll wait." Pete planted his feet. She looked tired, too tired to be lugging everything back to his house by herself. "Take what you have to, and I'll come back for the rest."

As feelings rushed over her, Anne dodged his stare. She didn't want him to be too kind, too thoughtful. Now more than at any time in her life, she needed to be strong, and he was making her aware of her aloneness, of her own vulnerability. A danger lurked near, a weakening in her to lean on him. Anne grappled for control with a reminder: Never rely on anyone too much. "On one condition," she said, resisting the emotional pull.

Pete paused while grabbing the high chair.

"I'm coming with only if you let me help with tonight's dinner."

Independent to a fault, Pete thought, as he collapsed the high chair.

While they carted the Portacrib and high chair over to his house, he played out some mumbo jumbo in his head about doing something noble. He knew it was all a bunch of bull. Had she looked like Frankenstein's bride or had a disposition like Lucrezia Borgia he wouldn't have been so quick with the invitation.

They stepped into his house to a phone that sounded like it was determined to ring off the hook. Pete rushed to answer it as Anne carried Rachel into one of the guest bedrooms.

His hello was greeted by the familiar voice of his brother. "It's been a long time," he said with uncertainty.

Pete tensed. "David, hi."

"I figured you were busy, but I thought I should give you a call. We have news," he said on a feigned lighter note. "Jimmy came over last night. He's getting married."

Pete couldn't say he felt happy for his youngest brother. He supposed he should. Neither of his brothers harbored the same unpleasant memories of their youth that he did. "Has he known her long?"

"Not too. But you know how love is."

He knew it could break a man.

"Anyway—he asked me to call you. The wedding is next month. Think you could come?"

Pete gauged the best approach as a strained silence hummed in the air. Sometimes little white lies suited the moment. "I'll try."

"We'd all like to see you," his brother added.

Pete shifted uncomfortably. "I'll let you know," he answered even as he searched for a good reason to stay away.

By the time he set down the receiver, he felt like hell. David knew he wouldn't come. During the past ten years, they'd rarely seen each other. Pete couldn't explain why that had happened. He only knew he'd wanted distance from them. He hadn't wanted to worry about anyone but himself. Now they had their lives, and he had his. It was better this way, he reassured himself, as he wandered into the kitchen.

Though eavesdropping wasn't something Anne condoned, it had been impossible not to overhear his phone conversation. Whoever David was, he'd awakened the same restrained and cool tone in Pete's voice that she'd heard when she'd stood at his back door last night. "I heard the phone ring."

He stood by the sink, drying wineglasses.

Anne noted there were only five. "A last minute cancellation?"

"No." As if his head were heavy, he raised it slowly. "My brother."

Anne managed to stifle a frown before it formed. "What can I do to help?"

"Everything is done."

"Done?" She followed his mood, telling herself to mind her own business. "You must be Supercook. What's in the oven?"

Pete wondered why she'd asked; she was already peeking into it. "Veal marsala."

"I'm impressed." She inhaled basil and lemon. "Do you cook often?"

"Rarely." Pete tugged his eyes away from the strain of denim at her backside. "I'm a fast-food addict."

She straightened. "Yet you're obviously a good cook."

An amused grin curved his lips. "Burger Haven," he said about a drive-through nearby, "is better. My car takes me there all the time." In fascination, he watched light dance across her hair with her movement. "Do you cook?"

"Nothing as elaborate as..." She started to gesture toward the oven, but then something caught her eye.

In the garbage can were containers bearing a large embossed Adolphi's on them. It was a quaint Italian restaurant best known for catering epicurean delights to private homes. Pete had the phone number memorized.

Disbelief and amusement flashed across her face. "You didn't cook tonight, did you, you phony?"

He heard a scolding quality in her voice, one he imagined her child might hear in years to come. "Or any night." He laughed and set down the fluted wineglass he'd been drying.

"Can you cook?"

"Does a peanut butter-and-jelly sandwich count?"

"If you're a ten year old it does. Bet you didn't even make the salad."

"Bet I didn't."

Curious now, she crossed to the refrigerator and opened it. There was little inside except several pizza cartons lining the shelves. She dared a peek in one of them, grimaced at the shriveled slice of pizza and

dumped the empty cartons into the garbage can.
"Where are the alfalfa sprouts?" she asked, eyeing the
large salad contained in one of Adolphi's crystal
bowls. "Adolphi's always puts them on the salads."

"Not on my salad."

She imagined John Wayne would have delivered
that line in the same tone. Tempted, she lifted the lid
of the pastry carton. "Ooh, cheesecake."

"A weakness?"

"Now you know my secret," she said, grinning back
at him.

Only one of many, Pete guessed. Squatting down,
he reached into the back of a bottom cabinet. He
hunkered back on his heels and held up one white and
one pale yellow candle. "Which ones?"

"White." She shot a smile at him. "What time is
your company coming?"

"Time..." With a quick glance at the clock, he
muttered a soft oath and charged from the room.

Soon, Anne deduced. She washed the few dishes in
the sink, then one by one, she opened cabinets to put
the dishes where they belonged. They could have gone
anywhere. Except for a lone frying pan and a few
plates and glasses, every cabinet was empty. His food
supply wasn't more plentiful. One cabinet near the
refrigerator held the mainstay of his kitchen staples: a
can of coffee, a bag of potato chips and an opened box
of cream-filled chocolate cookies.

He was a junk-food addict. That surprised her as
much as his admission about Burger Haven. In fact,
her first impression of him seemed drastically wrong

now. Little by little, she was beginning to see the man whom Karen had chanted praises about.

At the click of footsteps behind her, she closed the cabinet door. He'd showered and changed into a cable-stitch sweater and jeans that snugly hugged a masculine backside and muscular thighs. He'd *definitely* curl a woman's toes. Once more for good measure, Anne prompted herself that she didn't want to be that woman. She settled her hips back against the table. If she stayed at one end of the kitchen and he at the other, everything would be fine. "I wanted to talk to you about Mrs. Ashby. She mentioned baby-sitting, but I don't know her well enough. Is she responsible?"

He opened the oven door. "She could win a grandmother-of-the-year award."

Anne scratched off one problem. If she had to leave Rachel for a few hours, there was someone reliable nearby. "I liked her, but she . . . well, you might want to talk to her. She has the wrong impression about me, about Rachel. She told me the baby's father will get all that he wants."

Frowning, he strained to understand her.

Anne turned away to pour herself a cup of coffee. "She means *you*."

Amusement sprang into his voice. "That's ridiculous."

"I believe that's what I'm trying to tell you."

Instead of concern, he seemed amused. "I've learned it's useless to try and talk her out of anything. It doesn't work."

Anne shrugged. If he wasn't upset about what might become neighborhood gossip, she wouldn't be, either. "If there's nothing I can do, I'll leave you alone."

"You could stay." Pete started to reach for her but stopped himself.

Excitement Anne hadn't expected stormed her as she watched his eyes briefly fall upon her lips. Her heart beating a touch faster, she tried to laugh, to speak, but a pressure swelled up in her chest and blocked her air. In that instant, she knew how disruptive a force he could be.

She absolutely had to take control of her life again. Somehow she had to make Jerome listen. Somehow she had to stop his hateful anger. Somehow she had to find a way to leave Pete's home. With a stabilizing breath, she retreated a step. "No," she answered softly. "Thank you, but no."

Pete watched her leave. Though she'd uttered only a few words, she'd spoken volumes to him. Trust came slowly to this woman. She was saying no to more than his dinner invitation.

Now, all he had to do was listen.

Chapter Four

Within half an hour after Anne had wandered into the bedroom, the four walls started closing in on her. She liked being outdoors, jogging year-round, planting flowers in spring, shoveling snow in winter.

At home, she rarely sat still. She'd stocked up on aerobic tapes, not so enchanted with toning her body as keeping busy.

Pacing the room, she heard greetings and laughter. A lack of appetite hadn't made her refuse his dinner invitation. Oh, she could lie to herself and pretend that she'd believed favors should be returned. She could claim that she envisioned him explaining her to co-workers and wanted to save him discomfort. She could tell herself that he preferred a simple life-style, no complicated relationships, nothing that couldn't be explained quickly and easily, and she and Rachel never would fall into that category. She could try and fool herself, but why should she?

She'd refused him because she was attracted to him. Because he made her acutely aware of her femininity. Because he aroused dormant feelings inside her.

Restless, Anne circled the room for the third time, then paused at the closet. Friends always complained about sloppy boyfriends and husbands. The man in the other room was immaculate. At some moment, he'd emptied one of his dresser drawers for her, dumping summer shirts and shorts together in another one. A major concession for a man who seemed to slot a time and place for everything in his life.

Beneath plastic covers, summer suits all hung in a perfect row. Shirts, starched and pressed, followed. Ties on a rack were hung by color. And shoes . . .

Frowning, Anne squatted down. In a far corner of the closet were half a dozen jars filled with marbles. She smiled, wondering if they were a boyhood collection he'd treasured and kept, or a resurgence of the man's youth.

Again, he confused her. She'd met her share of different men. Each time her mother had married, she'd chosen a different kind of man as if that would guarantee success. It never had. But none of those men had ever seemed so enigmatic. The man she'd heard talking to his brother didn't sound like the kind who'd treasure anything from his past, especially a marble collection.

Anne closed the closet door, chiding herself for nosiness. She listened to the laughter from the other room and bent over Rachel to smooth out her blanket.

With a bored sigh, she groped in the diaper bag and blindly chose a book to read. With luck, it wouldn't be about a single mother finding Mr. Right. That, of course, was life's biggest fantasy.

Seated at the table, Pete grinned at friends and furnished monosyllabic answers at appropriate times, but thoughts of one woman intruded on his mind. Because of her, he stared into the blue eyes of a friend's wife and visualized enormous dark ones. He listened to voices and yearned to hear a distinctive smoky-sounding feminine one.

"Adolphi's veal is delicious, as usual," Martin said.

His wife, Cassie, nodded agreeably, her smile widening her round face. "This meal will kill my diet, Pete." Wholesome-looking, she constantly complained about battling bulges, a hazard of a kindergarten teacher who indulged in too many milk-and-cookie breaks. She broke into an anecdote about one of her student's propensity for fingerpainting with milk.

"Picasso, move over," Tim added humorously.

Beside him, his wife Jan's eyes gleamed with an impish sparkle. "That's better than what our son uses. He—" In midsentence, she stopped and gaped as a baby's cry drifted into the room.

Pete didn't have to wait long for more reaction. Heads snapped toward him. He felt like laughing at the look of incredulity on his friends' faces. Trying to keep the moment casual, he recounted his midnight visitor's situation. His explanation seemed useless. All eyes widened speculatively when Anne wandered into view with Rachel in her arms.

Almost nervously, she brushed a strand of hair away from her cheek with the back of her hand. "I'm sorry to interrupt." Patting Rachel to quiet her, she sent them a slim smile. "Someone's hungry."

When she disappeared, Martin chuckled softly. "Pete, when you play Good Samaritan, you certainly luck out."

His friends he could deal with. What bothered him more was the discomfort he'd seen in her eyes.

"She's very beautiful," Cassie said.

Pete nodded, thinking it ridiculous to deny the obvious. Even flustered with a look of apology in her eyes, she'd set off feelings in him. A tightness still coiling through him, he acknowledged that most men must feel something when they looked at her.

Beside him, Tim cleared his voice and gave him a knowing grin. "Now we know why the coffee tastes better tonight."

"Funny," Pete bantered good-naturedly.

"Face it, Pete. You make lousy coffee."

Looking out the kitchen window while she fed Rachel, Anne heard more laughter from the other room. Embarrassed, she wished the floor would open and swallow her. She damned the whole situation that had forced her to live like one of the homeless in some man's home.

The spoon scraped the bottom of the applesauce jar, and she offered the last mouthful to Rachel. From the other room, the bluesy sound of a sax mingled in with the voices.

Blowing out a long breath at her plight, Anne seized two of the chocolate cookies from the cabinet then slipped back into the bedroom unnoticed. She flopped onto the bed and resumed reading, determined to disregard everything but the characters in the story.

She must have dozed. The book still in her hands, she listened for voices. The house was quiet except for the sound of a mournful Reba McEntire coming from the kitchen radio.

Anne lay still. A dream about a fair-haired hero with wonderful blue eyes—a prince of a man who was sensitive and compassionate and strong and sexy—lingered in her mind.

That would have made sense except the hero in the romance possessed hair as dark as a raven's. The only fair-haired man with blue eyes that she knew was Pete. But she and he were like ships passing in the night. And there was nothing, absolutely nothing, romantic between them, she reminded herself, before slamming the book shut.

In the kitchen, yawning, Pete tied the plastic garbage bag. Grudgingly, he forced himself out the door for a dash to the garbage can. He should have had only one thought on his mind when he was trudging back to the house—falling into bed. Instead of sleep or his work, he wondered if Anne had slipped on that funky-looking orange jersey or something wispier. Was she sleeping? Was she having as much trouble as he was forgetting that she was within arm's length?

Every instinct he possessed cautioned him to back off. He usually had a tighter rein on his libido. For years, he'd walked alone by choice. Women he'd dated had understood he wasn't looking for more than fun and casual relationships. No way did Anne fall into that the same category. Fascinating as she was, she was the wrong type for him. He'd never met a woman with children who didn't view life seriously, too seriously.

But none of that seemed to matter when he opened the back door and saw her. Standing at the kitchen sink, she was sloshing a sudsy sponge across a plate. No makeup. Her hair messed. A pale blue robe clinging to her hips. Desire—so strong, his gut tightened with it—hit him.

She gave him a sleepy smile over her shoulder. "I thought you could use some help. Want to wash or dry?"

I want to know why I can't get you out of my head. With her movements, the V of her blue silk robe bellowed. Soft, pale flesh enticed him. As he caught the swell of her breast, his blood warmed even more, with a swiftness that shocked his system. Pete gritted his teeth and snatched up a dish towel. "I'll dry."

"Did I cause a commotion for you this evening?"

More than you know, he mused. "That was expected. Don't pay attention to any of them."

"I don't doubt everyone had a lot of questions." Bending forward, she dipped to her forearm into the sudsy water and searched for a spoon.

Her hair curtained her face. Were the strands as soft as they looked? he wondered. Would her skin feel so flawless beneath his fingers? The temptation to find out was too close. He sidestepped an urge with a move away toward the cabinet. "They're a nosy group. But Tim wants to thank you for saving him from my muddy brew. He should be used to it, though. He drank it all through law school."

She laughed because he'd smiled, not a stingy half smile, but a full one that bracketed the corners of his mouth with deep grooves. "You work for one of those fuddy-duddy corporate firms, don't you?"

Tugging open the silverware drawer, Pete nodded at the accuracy of her description. "Definitely."

"You should fit in."

Pete wondered if he should be insulted. "Do I look like a stuffed shirt?"

"Not at all. You look…" Anne clamped her mouth shut for a second. What foolishness was she about to utter? "I said that because you're one of the most organized men I've ever met." She motioned toward the neatly stacked silverware in the drawer. "Even that marble collection in your closet is organized by size." At the surprised glance he sent her, Anne was quick to add, "I saw them when I hung up a few things." The last thing she needed was him thinking she was a snoop.

He smiled wryly. "I didn't think you were pilfering my marble collection."

Shrugging, she wrinkled her nose. "I'm a little inquisitive sometimes. Did you begin collecting them when you were young?"

"No." He grabbed one of the plates on the drainboard. He felt himself being drawn to her as she tilted her head questioningly, interest sparkling in her eyes.

"About three years ago, I was reading a book about collectibles. Some marbles are worth thousands of dollars."

"You're one of those people," she teased.

She made him sound as if he were afflicted. "One of those people?"

"You know, someone who has to have a purpose or a good reason for everything."

He honestly didn't understand what was wrong with that.

"Were you so neat as a child?"

"Hardly," he answered, amused at how far off base she was. "I spent years sharing a room with kid brothers. Nothing was ever straight, because there was never enough room to hang clothes."

Anne pivoted and leaned back against the counter to give him her full attention. "Life wasn't simple, was it?" she asked, as she recalled her conversation with Norma about his beginnings.

"Having the bare necessities is a simple way of life."

"That's not what I meant."

No, he hadn't thought so.

"You didn't have it easy, did you?"

A slow smile lit his face. "Why all the questions?"

To say she was interested could be her downfall. "You know about me."

A laugh slipped into his voice. "Not a lot."

Anne heard more than humor in his voice. "More than I know about you."

His eyes narrowed at her as if trying to see beyond what was visible. "Okay. Fair is fair. Were you born here?"

Anne wagged her head. "Washington, D.C."

Pete arched a brow.

"My father was an administrative director of White House security. I don't remember any of that. My parents were divorced when I was young. Your turn," she said with a flip of her hand. "You were born in Denver?"

"In a different world."

Anne already knew how far he'd come. "And knew a lady named Lolita."

Pete shook his head in disbelief. "Norma talks too much."

Anne returned his smile. "She said very little. But I know you worked hard to get away from there."

"Hard enough. It was an uphill struggle, one worth all the effort. I took a lot of odd jobs. Dishwasher, obviously," he said, with a trace of lightness to keep the memories from darkening his mood. "There was never enough money. I was the oldest. I did anything to support them and get myself through school. I wanted that law degree badly."

"And your parents?"

"My mother died when I was thirteen. My father was gone long before he died." Pete stared into an empty cupboard, too much like the ones he'd known as a child. He remembered too many years when there was never enough of anything. "He fell apart after her death," he said, more to himself than her. "He thought alcohol helped. I'm not sure what he found in it. Maybe numbness. He was heartbroken when she died. In his mind, he'd lost the only person he'd ever loved."

"But he had you."

"Three of us. We reminded him too much of what he'd lost."

Anne's heart twisted for the boy he'd been, for the hurt he'd faced. What he wasn't saying carried more of an impact. After losing their mother, they must have needed their father desperately. While she'd endured her share of unhappiness in her childhood, she'd always had her mother. What he was talking about was total rejection. As he turned and his eyes met hers, she saw the tension in his features and the control he'd nurtured through the years. Opening an old wound hadn't been her intention. "You said there were three of you."

"I have two brothers," he answered, wondering if the call from David had bothered him more than he thought. He couldn't remember ever sharing so much with any woman.

Turning back to the sink, Anne watched the water swirl down the drain. She'd already guessed that he'd raised his brothers. He'd been no more than a child himself, and he'd become more father than brother, perhaps. "Do they live nearby?"

"Not too far away." Pete dodged more memories. "David is married. The other..." He paused and laughed, but Anne heard no joy or humor in it. "Jimmy's taking the plunge."

That he didn't approve was obvious. Anne couldn't blame him. He'd known a childhood that had carried more heartache than joy. "And you work for one of the better law firms."

"One of the best but—"

She looked back with a thoughtful expression. "But what?"

"Nothing ever runs smoothly." He took the last plate from her. "The higher echelon at the firm has a philosophy about what constitutes a reliable, stable image. Married men, according to Amos Klein, are more responsible."

She faced the sink again and sponged the outer rim. "Yet you're employed there."

"Employment isn't based on marital status. But my chances of being offered a partnership diminish because I'm not married."

Now that she knew his past, she doubted that set well with him. This man wasn't any more interested in marriage than she was. She was beginning to understand his obsessive ambition. He deserved the fruits of his labors, but if the law firm had such an archaic attitude about what constituted a suitable partner, his roadblock would be a difficult one indeed. He, too, must know that marriage at its best wasn't easy. Anne couldn't imagine any reason for trying it except love. Even that sometimes wasn't enough, even then sometimes the children suffered.

She stacked the six small plates, then stretched to place them on the shelf in the cupboard next to the bigger ones. "So you have almost everything you long for." As his hand brushed hers and pushed the plates onto the shelf, Anne looked up. He was close, so close that his breath warmed her cheek.

"Almost everything," he said quietly, feeling a tug-of-war inside him. He excused it as an emotional overload churned up by a phone call. But this moment seemed inevitable with her. He wanted to kiss her. He wanted to know her taste. He wanted to know if one kiss would end his preoccupation, his fascination with her.

When his eyes flicked to her mouth, Anne started to look away. Then he crowded her, and a gentle hand at the back of her neck held her still.

As his mouth slanted across hers, a longing she'd thought she'd never feel again descended on her. Slowly, thoroughly, his lips twisted over hers. She expected gentle. She felt demand. She expected her heart to pound harder. It raced. She thought his kiss might weaken her. It intoxicated. She never doubted that it would stir warmth. What she felt was heat.

The kiss changed so subtly, she was unprepared for her own response. She strained into him, her mouth hard against his lips, her tongue meeting and challenging his.

As he made her want, he made passion a part of her life again. She recognized the danger building and still didn't pull away. She'd thought she no longer hungered for this, but with nothing more than a kiss, he made her face herself honestly. She'd lied. She'd fooled herself.

She was a frustrated idiot, she thought disgustedly. What else could she be? Just because she'd missed desire didn't mean she had to give in to it.

In a desperate move, she twisted her face away from his. How had she fled from the danger of one man only to run toward someone who might prove more dangerous? "I'm sorry," she said breathlessly.

Despite her words, beneath his palm at her throat, her pulse pounded like a drum, beating out a different message. "I'm not."

Anne sidestepped him and took the retreating step that she'd failed to manage sooner. She could have stopped him. Why hadn't she? Dormant too long, the need for a man's embrace, for a kiss, had snuck up on her. She'd forgotten the power in that need, forgotten to remember she didn't want it complicating her life. On a quick turn away, she stretched for a deep breath. "That was nice but—"

Nice? Pete spun her around. "More than nice," he countered, still feeling the reeling sensation of the kiss.

Her heart pounding, Anne wanted to deny what she knew was true. It had been wonderful. "Pete..." His breath fluttered across her face, his lips too close again. "This makes no sense."

Arguing a point was his expertise. "It wouldn't, if you still loved him."

Oh, he was a master at zeroing in. Anne knew now never to underestimate him. "I don't need this." She presented her back to him and faced the bay window that partially viewed the street. What she saw outside froze her.

"You want me to pretend nothing happened?"

Anne couldn't think about them now. Fear was with her again. "Please leave me alone."

A step from her, Pete stopped cold. He stood for a second, dealing with the abruptness of her rejection. His ego wasn't so enormous that he couldn't handle a rebuff. If a woman shied away, he believed in a hands-off policy. But she'd given out a different signal.

Harder than he intended, he shoved away a chair in his path. It toppled over, clamoring as it hit the floor. He kept going.

He rarely lost his temper, and never with a woman. No woman had ever meant so much to him that he couldn't control his emotions. But with Anne, everything that had been was just that—a thing of the past.

As irritated with himself as he was with her, he strolled to the living room window. It was then that he saw the car passing by and the man staring at the Winslows' house. Something was wrong with Anne all right, but Pete surmised it had nothing to do with him. He charged back and found her frozen to the spot at the window. "The guy in the sedan—"

She jumped as if startled from private thoughts. "He drove by again?"

Pete saw her paleness. "Is he the private investigator?"

Anne wrestled to stay calm. "Yes."

"Who is your father-in-law?" he demanded.

"Jerome Barrett."

Pete knew the name. Barrett was an autocratic, influential man in the state, someone who didn't like any way but his own. And more important to Pete, Jerome Barrett was a close friend and a client of Klein's. "What happened yesterday?"

Distrust flashed in her eyes so quickly, he wanted to shake her.

"You're not alone this time—unless you want to be."

Had he spoken calmly, she might have rushed away, agitated and certain her problem wasn't his business.

But his anger reminded her that he had rights, too. She was in his home; he deserved to know why. "I was at work when the baby-sitter called. She'd sounded frantic as she told me that Jerome was at my house and wanted to see Rachel. I raced home. He demanded to see her. I wouldn't let him."

He deciphered the scope of her fear in the words wrenched from her. "I don't see the problem," he said honestly. "The courts won't take a child away from its natural mother."

Anne knew he was thinking logically. But logic had nothing to do with the panic inside her. "He never said he would go to court. He said there were other ways."

The real reason for her alarm reached him with the force of a punch. "Are we talking kidnapping? Did he make a move to take her?"

"No, he didn't touch her, but he said that he could provide Rachel with the kind of life she deserved. He could give her the best schools, the right social contacts . . . a world of difference."

Pete had already seen how devoted she was to her daughter. "I told you. Legally he can't do anything."

"He believes he's the right one to raise her," Anne said, struggling to keep her voice even.

Eyes, dark and shadowed with troubled thoughts, met his. There was more in her life, things she wasn't saying, but he sensed to tread gently.

"'What can *you* offer her?' he asked me." She paused, hearing the catch in her own voice.

"What did you say?"

"Love," Anne answered softly. Before her stood a practical man. Would he place the same importance on that emotion as she did? Would he realize how much more important love was for a child than money and prestige?

"I never expected the private investigator to find me." She shook her head. "That wasn't smart. I thought that I'd lost him, but he obviously learned Karen's new address." She sighed at her stupidity. "Of course, he'd check out all my friends."

Tense, she stood with her back ramrod straight as if ready to face a firing squad. He could offer her soothing words or a sympathetic embrace, but she was clinging by her fingertips against panic. What she needed most was sound reasoning. "Your car is in the Winslows' garage. He doesn't know you're here, Anne."

Anne heard him, but a moment passed before the truth in his words truly registered in her mind. Of course. He was right. The private investigator was watching Karen's house, not his. He deserved a thank-you for helping her hold on to a thread of calm. Another man would have embraced her, weakened her. How had he known what she needed, what she wanted most? That proved as unsettling as his kiss. She'd made her share of mistakes lately, she reflected. Accepting his home as a hiding place might top the list. Too easily, she could forget that her worries, her problems, her concerns weren't his, too. "I've decided to leave," she announced, not giving herself time to consider the decision.

"Where will you go?"

Anne watched his eyes shift to her lips. Memory of the kiss was still too near. "Home."

"It's not any safer now. So why are you going?" he demanded more than asked. "Because you're afraid?"

Uneasy, she breathed deeply. "That doesn't make sense. If I were afraid, I'd stay."

His gaze locked with hers. "That depends on what you're afraid of."

Anne stepped back slowly and turned away. What she felt like doing was running.

Chapter Five

Pete awakened the next morning to a fresh pot of coffee and Anne's thank-you note. Even before he'd rolled out of bed, he'd known she was gone. A quietness that was familiar but more nerve-racking than Rachel's cry surrounded him.

He didn't want to ponder why his home seemed so empty suddenly. He'd always led a life free of personal commitments because he'd been too immersed in his work to share his time. Privacy had mattered to him—so much so that despite a fondness for a few women, he'd never wanted to share his home with any of them. It made no sense to him that the very existence he'd strived for was troubling him this morning, but one thing was certain: he'd had a night like he'd never known before. One kiss had unbalanced him, a rarity for a man who usually commanded a tight rein on his emotions. The memory of her taste had haunted him. No, it had taunted him and made him too aware that one kiss would never be enough.

He reminded himself that he had an obsessive nature. When he wanted something, he was driven. That had been true of his ambition but had never pertained to a woman before. He'd desired, he'd pursued, but he'd never before yearned for something as simple as the sound of a certain woman's voice or the sight of her smile.

All day he dodged an impulse to call her. Yet he went so far as to pull out the phone directory and look up LeClare. There wasn't a single one listed.

He figured that was fate's way of telling him to forget about her. But the day dragged. He jogged, reviewed a hostile takeover by a client and munched on pizza while watching a Broncos game on television.

Over dinner, he reasoned with himself. She was leading a chaotic life. She had too much trouble. She had a baby. She was exactly the kind of woman he usually steered clear of. She already had a good reason to want the homey life-style with the house and white picket fence. He knew the pitfalls of a relationship with a woman like her.

Bounding from the chair, he crossed to the bedroom and the rowing machine. Under it, he found a pink rattle. In his bedroom, her perfume lingered faintly, her child's sweet powdery scent mingling in. Earlier, he'd spotted a tiny spoon by a kitchen chair.

He palmed the rattle, viewing the mementos left behind as fate's way of reconsidering. In all honesty, he'd never minded a little confusion or trouble. And if he were honest with her from the start, if she knew he never had any plans to hear a child call him Daddy, then why not see her again? What harm was there in enjoying her company for a little while?

For all her bravado during the previous evening, Anne spooked easily in her own home as fear that Jerome would return shadowed her. She never doubted she could handle a verbal confrontation with him. What worried her was Jerome bursting in and physically wrestling her for Rachel.

Edgy, she decided to clean. Above all, she needed to keep busy. While she dusted, she usually flicked up the volume on the stereo so the melodious tones of Whitney Houston or Barbra Streisand drifted through the rooms. Throughout the day, she worked to the rumbling of the washing machine.

As she scrubbed the kitchen floor, Anne kept an eye on Rachel kicking at the mobile of circus acrobats hanging in her playpen. Done by six, she considered curling up on the sofa with a book while Rachel slept, but at every creak, Anne jumped. With a disgusted sigh, she finally sank into a chair in Rachel's nursery to be close to her. The book lay in her lap while she stared at snowflakes rushing past the window and daydreamed about a kiss that had promised too much, too soon.

At seven the next morning, fresh flakes glistened on the tangled limbs of an oak tree outside her front door. Though the trip to Mrs. Ashby's was out of her way, Anne concluded that Rachel would be safest with her.

She reached the department store with five minutes to spare before a Monday-morning meeting and dashed across the parking lot. Winded, she breezed into and out of her office. Her secretary merely waved.

Three hours later, she left the think-tank session of all the store's buyers and retraced her steps to her office at a slower pace.

Linda greeted her with a frown. "The shipment of holiday fashions came in. The blue sequined Saint Laurent was missing."

Anne made a face. "Wonderful."

"Typical Monday morning," Linda said, trailing Anne into her office.

It was small, painted a muted mauve and furnished with a few comfortable pale green chairs. Anne had bought several plants, but the only personal touch was on her desk—a photograph of Rachel.

"Obviously I didn't get a chance to ask earlier. Is everything all right for you now?"

"It's about the same." Anne settled behind her desk. "My weekend plans were changed slightly. Instead of staying at Karen's, I was an uninvited houseguest of her neighbor. He was nice, but I couldn't stay there," she said as casually as she could.

Like a mother, Linda zeroed in on the mention of a male. "He?" She dropped to the chair across from Anne. "Who is he?"

Anne rifled through the messages Linda had just handed her. "Sir Galahad."

Linda inched forward on her chair. "This sounds intriguing."

Not deaf to the curiosity in her friend's voice, Anne gave her a dismissing wave. "Not really. I came back home yesterday."

"Married?"

"No."

"Then what . . . is he straight?"

Anne flipped through her Rolodex for the vendor's number. "And good-looking."

"Then what's wrong with him?"

It was a logical question. Most single women would jump at the chance to spend time with him. At Linda's continued inquisitive stare, Anne cautioned, "Don't let your imagination get away from you."

Linda beamed. "Not me."

Amusement rose within Anne at the understatement. Whenever possible, Linda and Karen had been urging every bachelor they knew toward her. "Of course not you. Even though you are an incurable romantic."

"I believe somewhere there is a right person for everyone. It's destiny."

Anne couldn't help but laugh at the ridiculousness of the moment and the fact that she was caught up in romantic girl talk despite some weighty problems in her life.

"Could I ask his name?"

"Pete. Pete Hogan."

"Oh, *the* Pete Hogan. Karen mentioned him. He's a lawyer, isn't he?" She went on. "Handsome and charming and obviously chivalrous. Sounds perfect."

Anne remained silently noncommittal. How many times had her mother thought some man was perfect for her and learned differently?

"You *have* had an interesting weekend."

"Too interesting," Anne said, picking up the telephone to dial the vendor about the missing dress.

She glanced at the clock and considered calling Norma again then resisted the thought. She'd already called her four times and four times had been assured that Rachel was all right.

Through what was left of the morning, Anne closeted herself in her office with a pot of hot tea and stacks of receipts. Then she handled a late delivery on a special order and sat through a quick meeting about spring merchandise. After circulating through the departments to learn the status of sales merchandise, she raced back to her office.

Glancing at her wristwatch, Anne breezed past Linda's desk to make a telephone call to a vendor.

Linda's smirk should have warned her.

Anne reached her office doorway and stilled. On her desk was a small bouquet of spring flowers. She hadn't expected this, she realized. He didn't give the impression of being a man who believed in romance. Bracing herself, she picked up the card; a house key slid into her palm. It was a gift that carried far more meaning than the flowers.

Over Anne's shoulder, Linda read, "'This is the only key I could find for you. You know the address.'" Linda beamed. "Are they from Pete?"

Anne prayed heat wasn't flushing her face. She set the flowers on her credenza and moved quickly to her chair. Seated, she felt steadier. "It's a joke."

"It's rather romantic."

"There's nothing romantic about it. He was making a joke," she said emphatically.

"Anne, you need a man."

"That's an anachronism," she quipped back.

"No, it isn't. No one should be alone," Linda insisted firmly before leaving the room.

Anne fingered a petal on a flower. She had once thought that, too, but not anymore. Maybe, if her life had taken a different turn, she'd believe differently, but she'd spent too many years watching her mother seeking that dream and never finding the right man.

And when Anne had tried, she'd failed, too.

Once was enough for her.

By two, she'd read his note half a dozen times. He was offering her a way to escape more troubled days because of Jerome, but Anne saw a different kind of danger if she accepted.

Bending her head, she concentrated on the sales figures for a trendy black-and-white outfit. Her good intentions to stop wasting time lasted less than five minutes.

She raised her head as she heard the lilting strains of a violin. Tranced, Anne visually followed a tuxedoed violinist's ingress into her office. While the music of Beethoven filled the room, a thin waiter with grizzly gray hair pushed a cart laden with silver platters through the doorway. He beamed and displayed a salad piled high with alfalfa sprouts, meant to feed five people.

Anne stifled a laugh. A second platter held a peanut butter-and-jelly sandwich. On the third platter was the pièce de résistance, an enormous slice of the richest-looking cheesecake she'd ever seen.

She sagged back in her chair. Who'd have thought Pete Hogan had a silly side?

"He's full of surprises," Linda said later after the men had left.

Anne swiveled her chair away from the window and the view of delicate-looking dancing snowflakes. "I'm doing just fine on my own."

Linda looked unconvinced.

"You think I'm mouthing the right words at the right moments?"

"A lot of single mothers claim they can handle a career and raise a family and don't need any man. It's the feminists' spiel. Aren't you a little lonely? Don't you miss being married?"

Miss it? She hadn't allowed herself to consider the question before this. Yes, she did miss the warmth of a man beside her. She missed tenderness and loving someone special. She missed having someone whom she could share joys and worries about Rachel with, but she also recognized the fragility of marriage, the heartache it could bring to a child.

She frowned at the cheesecake crumbs on the plate before her. Another man would have sent her lunch from an expensive French restaurant. Pete hadn't been trying to impress her. When he'd chosen what to send her, he'd had but one thought—to make her smile.

He'd succeeded, but only because she hadn't been romanced in so long. More than once, he'd caught her off guard. That wouldn't happen again. She wasn't a sentimental, romantic twenty-year-old easily bowled over by flowers and a silly lunch.

While driving toward Norma's later that day to pick up Rachel, she convinced herself that even his kiss hadn't been special. She'd simply overreacted to it, to the softness she'd heard in his voice, to the implied compliment of his interest.

With the furnace at Karen's out of commission, Anne decided to repack her car. She pulled up to the curb in front of Norma's and slipped out of her good coat and into a winter jacket. She made a quick stop at Norma's then hurried to Karen's.

Pete spotted her carting boxes out of the Winslows' house. Fate was playing him another hand, he decided, as she came back out minutes later, struggling with the baby's swing. It seemed reasonable to him that she needed a little neighborly help. It was also as good an excuse as any to see her again.

He regarded himself as pragmatic, a man with an inordinate amount of common sense, but he couldn't stop himself from trying to push their relationship beyond friendship. He'd already decided he needed to ease her out of his mind or learn more about her. Either way, he'd get back the control he hadn't known since she'd first said a breezy "hi" to him.

He grabbed his parka and headed for the door. Though the florist's delivery had required only a phone call, the silly lunch had taken more effort. He hadn't minded one bit, deciding if he couldn't forget her then he'd be damned if he'd let her forget him.

Stuffing the last of Rachel's clothes into a bag, Anne drew a long breath. Two more loads, and she'd be done. She propped the folded playpen against a kitchen wall and felt some satisfaction. She hadn't thought about Pete even once during the past half hour. A good sign, she thought smugly.

"Need help?"

Startled at the sound of a male voice, she nearly dropped the jar in her hand. Her stomach muscles tensed. A thrill that seemed terribly adolescent rippled through her as he smiled. How could she have been so confident seconds ago? she wondered.

"I saw you when I came home," he said, closing the door behind him.

For a moment, his eyes met hers. The unwavering stare left her breathless as the memory of his kiss seemed to whisper in the air between them. "I only have these to pack," she managed and gestured toward the soap cabinet. "And there are a few things to carry out, like the playpen."

Unsettled, she scooted around the table and passed him, stepping outside for a carton. Wind ruffled at her hair and nipped at her cheeks with its wintry chill. She needed the coldness. Heat was with her again. The heat of excitement, of anticipation. "Thank you for the flowers and—"

He took a step outside the doorway to join her, and with a subtle shift, blocked the cold. "Did you like them?"

"Well, yes." That wasn't what she'd planned to say. But she had been thrilled with them, amazed he'd found a florist to provide the lure of springtime in the middle of autumn. "About the flowers."

"You already thanked me."

Anne skirted past him in the doorway and dropped the empty cartons to the floor. With a look back, she watched him slip off his jacket and nearly moaned. She had to get a grip on this, but it wasn't going to be easy. Stupidly, she'd forgotten the pride and tenacity he possessed that had helped him rise from his beginnings and become such a successful man. "And the lunch was . . . unusual."

Grinning, he hunkered down in front of the soap cabinet. "Did it please you?"

She could hardly lie. A reluctant smile warmed her voice. "Yes, I liked it."

"Disregarding the alfalfa sprouts, I thought it would be good." He paused. "That's interesting, isn't it?"

Anne sensed a danger in agreeing with anything he said. "What's interesting?"

"That we have so much in common."

Anne recalled the neatness in his house and the disorder that usually prevailed in her own. "We have *nothing in common*," she said, laughing.

He went on as if deaf to her denial, "And while I'm not a big reader of popular fiction . . ."

Anne slitted her eyes to look down at him. When had he noticed the books she'd stuffed into Rachel's diaper bag?

"I enjoy an evening listening to music and reading. What do you like to do?"

"What do I like to do?" Anne paused in reaching for a baby jar on the top shelf, too aware where the direction of his question could lead them.

"Dance? Bowl? What?" He knew he was confusing her. He was confusing himself, too. At some moment, maybe after he'd kissed her, or after she'd left his home, or after he'd awakened to find her thank-you note, he'd begun craving for more time with her. He just hadn't known how badly he'd desired that until this moment.

A fluttery sensation coursed through her. Uncertainty? Yes. And excitement. He could bring too much of both into her life if she wasn't careful. "Swim. We joined a swimming class."

"Who's 'we'?" Pete asked, remembering that somewhere there was a man named Michael.

"I went with Rachel."

"With Rachel?"

"They give swimming lessons to babies now."

"Sounds like a smart idea.

"I thought so. And Rachel had fun."

"Did you?"

The unexpected question threw her off balance for only a second. "Are you trying to say that I'm neglecting myself?"

"Only you know if that's true."

She sent him a mild look, then resumed shifting around the jars in the box to make room for others. "I belong to a health club. I visit friends. I play tennis and the guitar. You're the one who puts in a workaholic's hours. Not me," she added pointedly, while rising to her toes for a jar at the back of a cabinet. "But I'm not some twenty-year-old with no responsibilities. I'm a mother. I have someone else who relies on me to make decisions—the right decisions."

"You're doing just fine," he assured her. His eyes followed the movement of her body as she stretched. "You're a terrific mother."

Anne stilled. He could have told her she was beautiful. He could have praised her success as a buyer for Lindsen's. He could have raved about her kiss. But she'd have taken nothing to heart as much as what he had said.

"When is your day off?"

"My day off?" Anne was still frowning that he'd so effortlessly stroked her soft spot.

He laughed. "You're repeating yourself."

What she was really doing was acting like an idiot, she mused.

"It doesn't matter. This week I'm adaptable. Any day is fine."

"A ridiculous statement from a workaholic." She picked up a box of laundry soap, then put it back, remembering it was Karen's, not hers.

"Would you believe I'm changing my ways?" At her skeptical look, he laughed. "A little. And I know a great place where you can get alfalfa sprouts on hamburgers."

"Sounds disgusting."

Humor filled his voice. "I thought it would tempt you."

Setting down the bottle of spot cleaner she held in her hand, she wondered why he was being so persistent. "Pete, listen. You have your life mapped out. I don't know where mine is going right now."

"That's temporary, isn't it?" he asked softly.

She sighed. "Oh, I hope so."

He pushed to a standing position. "So give me another reason."

Slowly she counted to a slow ten, too aware she wasn't frightened of him but of herself. Despite her resistance, when his arms had wrapped around her, when his mouth had met hers, she had responded. "I'm not interested in—"

"Me?" He stood on the opposite side of the table and felt like miles separated them.

"In any of this," she said, unable to get the one word out that would stop him. The denial sounded flat even to her own ears.

Pete wasn't stupid. He knew why she was resisting. She smiled, laughed, pretended, and underneath it all, she harbored an enormous amount of wariness and distrust. What could he say? All he knew was that he liked her smile. He liked the throaty way she laughed.

A touch unsteady, Anne watched him skirt the table.

Pausing beside her, he brushed a thumb across the curve of her jaw.

Though never a game player, she could think of no way to stop him except one—maybe. She tried her hand at besting him. Certain he was used to dates inclined toward elegance, she chose an answer to stop him cold. "I've always liked ice skating."

Laughter crept into his voice. "Ice skating?"

"Do you ice-skate, Counselor?"

At the dare penetrating her voice, amused, he went along with her. "I used to play hockey."

A distinct sense of being outmaneuvered again drifted over Anne. "Hockey?" she repeated uneasily.

"I played a lot of hockey when I was a kid," he said, unable to resist touching her hair. In fascination, he watched one dark curl coil around his finger. "It got me in less trouble than throwing snowballs from the tops of the roof."

Anne's shoulders sagged. Why was he always one step ahead of her? "Did you walk a fine line when you were young?"

"Something like that. But I tried to stay out of trouble. Hockey helped." She smelled wonderful to him. She felt wonderful, he thought, as his fingers skimmed the curve of her neck. "Sometimes the easiest, and as far as police were concerned, safest way to even scores was by playing football or hockey. An elbow could jab an eye without the authorities getting wise."

Anne tsked.

"Bet you were a good little girl," he teased, pleased at the smile in her eyes.

She could have told him she had to be. Her mother had demanded it. Her stepfathers had expected it. "Yes, I was."

"They say opposites attract."

His face was too close, the memory of his kiss upon her again as his fingers stroked the back of her neck. A faint shock wave shot down her spine like a warning. "The kind that stayed away from troublemakers."

Humor accompanied his words. "Like me?"

He gave her an affronted look that made her smile. "I'm still trying," she said pointedly, but instead of a cool tone, she sounded breathless, as if she'd run several blocks.

"I'm respectable now. Responsible. You said so."

In a suit and perfectly knotted tie, he'd looked like the epitome of respectability, but at the moment, wearing a midnight blue sweater and snug Levi's, his hair tossed from the wind, he conveyed a tougher, more dangerous, impression. She noted the small scar at the bridge of his nose and raised a hand to touch it. Midway she stopped herself. Too late. His hand captured hers. Anne felt a surrender taking place within her. "Did you get that playing hockey?" she managed.

"A girl I was dating in high school got mad and tossed a book at me. Landed perfectly to do damage."

"You do date interesting women."

Pete turned her palm up and kissed it. "I try."

Heat spiraled up her arm. Anne struggled as she'd struggled since they'd met and slid her hand free of his.

As she stepped around him, Pete resisted an urge to grab her. "I'll meet you," he said to her back. With some satisfaction, he watched her pace falter. "Then you won't have to think of it as a date."

She couldn't explain why she stopped. Maybe because of the edge of exasperation she heard in his voice. Maybe because a little voice inside her told her to. Maybe because youthful anticipation rippled through her. "I don't have a sitter."

"Rachel can go ice skating, too."

Anne turned a dumbfounded look on him to see him curling an arm around the folded playpen. "Rachel can what?"

He stopped at the door and grinned in a confident way she was becoming familiar with. "You'll see."

Weak as water, Anne berated herself.

Chapter Six

All the next day, Anne debated with herself. It wasn't a date. She was meeting a friend after work to go ice skating. But with every mile she drove closer to Norma's, her mind ridiculed her for fooling herself. She was going on a date. She hadn't been on a date in years. What would they talk about? Would he kiss her again?

She must be crazy, she decided, when she entered Norma's house. Sitting at the kitchen table with a cup of coffee, Pete Hogan exuded the calm confidence of a man who had everything planned. Anne was definitely "winging it."

"I hope they fit," he said, dangling ice skates.

The last time she'd worn a pair, she'd been eleven years old. Her backside had glided over the ice more than her feet. "I'll probably break my neck. I'm not

Olympic material." Anne looked for Norma. "I wonder if Rachel still has the sniffles."

Standing, Pete gave her no room to beg out. "She's fine." Before she managed some excuse, he urged her forward. "Norma's getting her ready."

The pond was crowded with families. Despite his protests, Anne insisted on driving her own car. While lacing her skates, she envied a girl about eight years old whizzing by. In the next few minutes, she was about to make a fool out of herself.

At the frown wrinkling her brow, Pete could think of a dozen things he'd prefer to be doing with her. Ice skating wasn't one of them. But she was a woman who'd give nothing without trust, and winning that required a pace Pete was finding frustratingly slow. "You don't look happy to be here. You suggested ice skating," he reminded her.

Anne paused in lacing her skates and drilled him with a withering stare. "Don't look so smug. You know I did that because I didn't think you could ice-skate."

Amusement glinted in his eyes. "Do I look klutzy?"

The fact was he looked athletic, but she'd thought he'd be more inclined to enjoy a different type of sport. "I thought you'd like racquetball or golf."

Deftly he crisscrossed her laces. "I do."

"Yes, but ice skating isn't usually on the uprising young executive's list of pastimes."

A slow smile formed on his lips. "Well, I'm not usual." Pete drew her to a stand with him.

"I'm beginning to realize that," she mumbled. She heard his chuckle but decided to ignore it. He'd already gotten the upper hand more than once.

Inching onto the ice with him, in fascination Anne surveyed the unique sled he'd found for Rachel. Bundled in a snowsuit and several blankets, Rachel fit snugly in a cushioned seat on a sled with a buggy handle for pushing. As a father and small son glided by, she tilted her head to watch them, her eyes round with delight. "Where did you get this sled?" Anne asked as she wobbled on her blades.

With one hand on the sled handle, he offered his other arm to her for support. "Every friend I know has kids. I figured someone would know about something like this."

Her gaze fixed on her feet as if they were foreign to her, she grasped his arm as a lifeline and shuffled forward, feeling like a toddler taking her first steps. "I'm terrible at this."

"You're doing fine."

"Not too good." She squealed as one foot slipped away from her. Beneath her hand, Pete's arm tensed to bear her weight and stop her. "I'm going to take you down with me sooner or later."

"I'll take my chances." He leaned closer and kissed the bridge of her nose. "You look cute."

"I look twelve years old." Night air stinging her face, she tugged her knit cap lower over one ear. "I thought you didn't like winter."

"I like it." His smile came quickly. "Everything about it except for shoveling snow. Hate to do that. It was the first job I had as a kid. I'd come home from school, wanting to play hockey, and I knew I had what seemed like miles of sidewalks to shovel before I could meet the guys.''

''I had it easy.''

''Then, but not now.''

''Now isn't so bad,'' she said with an optimism that had aided her through some previous difficult times. ''I didn't work until I was eighteen.'' As snow flurries filtered down, she snuggled deeper in her parka. ''There was never a need to. My family had enough money. I remember I wanted to take a job one summer as a salesclerk.''

''Why?''

Anne slanted a brief look away from her skates. ''Why what?''

''Why would you want the job if you didn't need it?''

''To make my own money.''

''You were born with that independent streak, huh?''

Anne squared her shoulders dramatically. ''Yes.''

Pete thought about the years he'd worked so hard just to put food on the table. Never having a lot of free time to himself, he couldn't imagine anyone willingly giving it up. ''So why wouldn't your mother let you?''

''She had the summer planned. I was to stay at an aunt's while she and her latest husband attended a business course in Boston.''

Pete latched on to the key words. ''Latest husband?''

''She had many. She stayed with my father far longer than either of them wanted to be together. Ten years. All for the sake of his career. They finally divorced when I was four. I hardly remember my father. He remarried quickly to a woman as ambitious as him."

She spoke easily, almost mechanically, but Pete heard a world of hurt in her voice. "Your father never saw you?"

Having opened the door, Anne knew he'd resist letting her close it. "He was busy with his career, with a new wife. He remembered to send a check on my birthday and Christmas. I knew the housekeepers better than I knew my parents."

"What about your mother?"

She sent him a semblance of a smile. "My mother found another man who was just as intelligent and successful as my father had been. That marriage didn't last, either. Neither did my father's second one. That was divorce number two for each of my parents. My father seemed to learn from his mistakes. Two marriages, two divorces were enough. He was really married to his career. But my mother didn't learn anything. She married again—two more times."

Anne met the intense blue eyes trying to see inside her. "Every time I began to depend on a new father sticking around, my mother divorced him. They were all too preoccupied with their own lives to find room for other people. People like that don't really have time for a child, either."

Pete knew she thought he was one of those people, too.

"But I never stopped wanting a father." A child's despair seeped into her voice. "So I kept expecting too much from them. All except the last one. I wasn't a child anymore. I understood that promises, especially marriage promises, meant nothing, and would never include a father.''

Suddenly he wasn't sure he wanted to hear more. Had she asked, he couldn't have denied that he was as single-minded about his career as her parents had been about their own. And children weren't part of those plans.

"I married, certain I'd never break the vow I was making." Sadness filtered into her voice again. "Eventually I did."

"You divorced him before he died?"

"I'd planned to," she said softly.

Pete negotiated them around the ice pond one more time then steered her toward the edge. No psychology degree was necessary for him to understand that her childhood pain had made her stay with her husband, had urged her to preserve her marriage. It wasn't difficult to imagine that life with her husband had gotten unbearable. He didn't think she'd have called it quits otherwise. But she was still beating herself up for walking out the door. "So you failed once."

Her chin lifted a notch to meet his stare. "And never again," she said firmly, recalling the months she'd endured of Keith's drinking, his moodiness, his erratic behavior. "I won't put my daughter through the same kind of heartbreak that I went through as a child. I won't let her be hurt."

"There are never any guarantees, Anne."

"I'm not looking for any." Anne sighed as he guided the sled toward a snowbank. Her calves mushy, her ankles wobbly, she clutched on to his supporting arm and inched onto stable ground then bent over to check on Rachel. Her cheeks were rosy, her eyes bright.

"Tired?" he asked in response to Anne's sigh.

"From too much talking," she said with a deliberate lightness, and she began unlacing her skates. "I didn't mean to ramble like that."

He dropped to a knee to finish the task for her. He'd learned plenty and felt a sadness for a little girl who no one had paid attention to. She was wrong; they shared a lot in common. "I wanted to know more." He rose and drew her up with him. Initially he'd thought it wise to stay clear of her. Since then, he'd learned more about her. And now, he knew she wanted nothing permanent, either. Pete couldn't see any reason why they shouldn't be together.

While he loaded the sled into the trunk of his car, he watched her hurry to buckle Rachel into her car seat. She was planning a quick goodbye. He wasn't. All day, he'd been thinking about moments alone with her again. He wanted to kiss her again, knew he hadn't imagined the heat or the need. Before she reached the driver's side of her car, Pete closed the distance and caught her arm. "One minute."

Anne froze and slowly turned to face him. He stood practically on top of her. As he placed a palm on the car near her shoulder, she was trapped by more than his body. The need to be held, to be wanted, was with her again. But even before his head lowered, she knew she wasn't any more ready for his kiss than she had been. She placed a hand against his chest to keep some distance between them, but as his mouth closed over hers, her hand against his chest went limp.

Despite the coldness stinging her face and flapping at her jacket, she couldn't think of anything but him— his taste, the pressure of his mouth, the warmth of his hand at the back of her neck. With a will of its own, her body leaned closer, seeking the heat of his.

In that one instant, all the protests that she'd given him meant nothing to Pete. He'd seen pleasure sparkling in her dark eyes seconds before they'd fluttered and closed, and as he deepened the kiss and his tongue sought the sweetness within, he heard her soft moan.

He'd meant to steal a quick kiss. Just as quickly, he'd forgotten his intention. An overwhelming urge for intimacy trembled through him. He wanted to lose himself in this woman. It didn't matter that snow-flakes fluttered down on them, that the chill in the air rushed around him. Warmth blazed within. It didn't matter that her hand pressed to his chest to push him away. The caress of her other one on his face riveted him to her. This is what he'd been yearning for again. Yet it wasn't enough. He knew he wanted more, much more.

Anne tore her lips from his. "This isn't supposed to happen," she said, breathing hard, and scooted behind the steering wheel of her car. "It's too fast."

She was wrong. Pete hooked a hand over the top of the door to halt her from closing it. He'd known other women for months and hadn't felt such desire. He wanted to be with her. But there was more. For the first time in his life, he craved to be with a woman.

Pete didn't give himself time to consider why that need was consuming him. "No, you want this, too."

Staring at the dark dashboard, tightening her grip on the steering wheel, her heart pounded. "I'll admit I'm attracted to you, but I'm not interested in promises of forever from anyone."

Pete wanted to shake her. They were a breath away from reaching out to each other. She needed his embrace; he wanted hers. "Look at me."

Moonlight slanted across his face, revealing a confusion and desire in his eyes that reminded her too much of her own. "That doesn't mean you can't have anything," he said softly.

For a long moment, Anne just stared at him. She wasn't naive. She understood what he was saying. No ties, no promises.

She flicked on the ignition. Despite the rumble of the engine, all she could hear were his last words.

He didn't say them again. During the next three days, he came to her office and took her to lunch. He introduced her to Burger Haven. He became such a part of her day that she began to anticipate something as simple as a phone call from him.

She wished she didn't enjoy herself so much or smile so much when with him, but making such a wish sounded stupid. When with him, she didn't glance around, wondering if Jerome was near. She had fun. That amazed and surprised her almost as much as what hadn't happened. He hadn't kissed her again. As if letting her lead, he kept the distance she'd wanted from him and now yearned to close.

The light of day didn't help. The night before had
proven difficult. A movie, pizza and then a quick
good-night at the door. He'd turned away without
even trying to kiss her. And he'd left her dreaming
about it, aching for it.

She was also yearning for the familiar surroundings of her own home. She'd spent only two nights,
two restless nights at home, then had begun shifting
from one friend's house to another. Her cowardliness
didn't please her. Besides not enjoying intruding on
friends, when they'd met Pete, she'd caught too many
speculative smiles. After almost a week of a vaga-
bond's life-style, Anne decided enough was enough.
Tomorrow, she and Rachel were going home.

At eleven-thirty the next morning, Pete whizzed into
his office after a morning meeting with an argumen-
tative couple who couldn't agree about the benefici-
aries on their will. The husband and wife weren't his
clients, but Klein had insisted he be present. Pete
viewed the request as a good sign. The firm's partners
often sat in on other lawyer-client consultations.

An obligation on his mind, for the next hour, he
punched phone numbers on Lolita's behalf. The Hu-
mane Society cooperated, but bureaucratic red tape
stalled him when he called the Licensing Department.
Twenty minutes passed of getting the runaround before Pete had answers to his questions.

"I thought you weren't here," Tim called out from
the doorway. Beet red from the cold, his face looked
puffy. "I stopped by your office earlier."

"I decided to take a late lunch today. Are you all done?"

Tim nodded. "Jan has a bee in her bonnet about lowering my cholesterol. I tried this godawful health food place three blocks over. You didn't miss anything."

Pete nudged back his chair and strode toward the coat rack near the door. He'd made plans, too, for lunch. Where to go remained questionable. But he knew with certainty he wouldn't be alone. "I heard that Frank brought in a new client."

"Megabucks client. Anything to get Klein's attention. You need to do that."

Pete shoved an arm into the sleeve of his overcoat. "I don't know any millionaires looking for legal service."

"Jan and I thought about it. Klein would lean in your favor if you announced that you were going to get married. Now, Jan has a friend—"

Pete raised a halting hand. "Not interested."

"Jeez, Pete, think about the job."

"I'm not jumping into marriage just for the sake of a job."

"This is a nice woman. A schoolteacher."

"Loves children?"

"Yeah."

Pete looked up from buttoning his coat. "No thanks."

Tim released an exasperated sigh as Pete stepped around him. "Where are you going to find a woman who doesn't want them?"

Without a glance back, Pete shrugged and headed for the elevator. More important to him was what was he going to do about his undeniable attraction to a woman who already had one.

Lunchtime raced in on her. Anne nibbled on one of the stale saltines she'd dug out of a bottom desk drawer and she skimmed a finger down one more column of an inventory sheet. Though not hungry, she needed a break. She hunched to ease stiff shoulder muscles, and with a walk in mind, she reached down for her purse.

The intercom buzzed like the drone of bees. Laughing, Anne looked up to tease Linda about a heavy finger on the button. Instead of her, Jerome stood in the doorway.

Hovering close behind him, Linda insisted, "He wouldn't wait."

Anne geared herself for another confrontation and signaled Linda away with a wave.

Jerome viewed it as his cue. He took two steps closer to her desk and demanded to know where Rachel was. "She belongs with me," he said angrily. "You can't hide her. My man told me you've been at that Winslow woman's house and who knows where else, but I'll find her."

Somewhat naively, Anne had never expected him to storm into her office. "Oh, yes, I've seen your private investigator, who by the way doesn't deserve what you're paying him," she said in a calm voice that she hoped hid her anxiety.

"He isn't used to someone so cunning. My son wasn't, either," he retorted hotly. "He didn't realize that all you wanted was the money."

Anne's temper rose. "We had very little because you spoiled him so badly that he didn't know how to hold on to any job."

His face reddening, he drilled a look at her as if she were something vile. "Lies just flow from your mouth, don't they?"

Anne motioned toward the door while she warred with herself to keep an edge of hysteria out of her voice. "Leave now. Right now before I call the police."

"Do you think you're a match for me? Missy, I'm Jerome Barrett. I slice down men bigger than you."

No meeting with him ever left her unscathed. He drained her with his accusations, his anger, his hate. Anne straightened her back, refusing to weaken in front of him and skirted her desk to meet him head-on. "I want you to leave. I don't know why you came here, but—"

"Oh, I'll tell you why I'm here."

Pete tugged off his gloves and unbuttoned his overcoat before opening the door to Anne's office. He'd spent three days trying to thread trust between them. Though he sensed she'd enjoyed herself with him, he didn't fool himself. She was frightened of involvement. Hell, he was just as apprehensive. He started out thinking desire, aching for her. Now, a day without her seemed too long. And he was still aching for her.

As the door closed behind him, a slim brunette at the desk perched her glasses on the center of her nose and peered over the top of them at him.

Why she didn't smile became clear as a male voice elevated in anger. The door to Anne's office flung open. "Don't forget what I've said," a gray-haired man yelled as he marched out.

No introduction was needed. As the owner of Barrett's, a statewide department-store chain, Jerome Barrett's photograph often graced the business and society sections in the newspaper.

Out of the corner of his eye, Pete saw Anne's secretary closing a hand over the telephone receiver. "I'm calling Security," she announced.

Pete rounded her desk. "You won't need to. He's leaving," he added with a quietness he knew was more intimidating than if he'd raised his voice.

Jerome whirled toward him. "Are you a friend of hers?" He pointed a finger at Pete, then his eyes narrowed in a deciphering manner as if to see Pete more clearly. "We've met before."

Pete held silent though he could have reminded Jerome that they'd been introduced in Klein's office last summer.

Puzzlement clouded Jerome's eyes, but he gave his head a barely perceptible shake as though trying to banish his own confusion. "Be smart and stay clear of her. She's to blame for my son's death. Ask her," he demanded. "If she had been a better wife, my son would be alive today."

Anger and a desire to play that damn knight knifed through Pete again. Taking a step to the side, he placed himself between Jerome and Anne's office. "Leave."

Jerome's eyes riveted on him. "Whoever you are, you're a damn fool."

Slumped against the doorjamb of her office, Anne waited until the main office door closed behind Jerome with an earth-shattering slam. "Now you've met Rachel's grandfather."

She forced a smile. "Are you all right?" he asked.

"I'm fine." Of course she wasn't. Nerves were jumping, her legs felt weak and her heart was still racing.

"I came to take you to lunch. Where's your coat?"

Anne was too exhausted to argue with anyone else. More than anything, she needed to get out of the building and feel the crisp cold of the wind hitting her face.

She was grateful for his silence during the elevator ride. He seemed to sense her need for time to sort through the consequences of what had just happened.

Lowering her head against the snowflakes flying at her face, she fixed her eyes on her boots, on the sidewalk slick with icy snow. "I'm not really hungry."

With an unmistakable tenseness, her back seemed to draw forward. Vulnerability clouded her eyes despite an attempt at a smile. "Then we'll walk," he said, willing to give whatever she needed. While they window shopped, dozens of questions barraged his mind. Share it with me, he wanted to say to her, but he remained quiet.

Outside an antiques store, Anne paused. It brought back days when she'd been far along in her pregnancy. Caught up in his own grief then, Jerome hadn't bothered with her. She'd spent hours walking during those days, trying to free her mind of regrets. She'd browsed often in stores just like this one. Feeling a desire to recapture the peace she'd felt before, with her baby safe and stirring inside her, she urged, "Let's go in."

Pete curled his fingers over her shoulders as she started to step away. He couldn't go on with this pretense that nothing was wrong. "What happened in your office?"

As his grip tightened stubbornly, her body went soft against him. "More angry words."

Lightly he touched her hair then turned her in his arms to face him. "Talk to me." He wanted to comfort her, bring back her smile.

"I didn't understand what he was saying at first," Anne said softly. "But he kept repeating that he was a rich man, that he could travel constantly if he had to. He could disappear if he wanted to, and no one would find him." Despite efforts not to, her voice broke, "No one could find him or Rachel."

"He's dangerous, Anne."

She welcomed the biting wind snapping at them and breathed the cold air into her lungs. "He's hurting. Confused and grieving," she said quietly. "I do understand. I believe he wants Rachel because he's clinging to a part of Keith that's still alive."

Alarming her wasn't his intention, but Pete felt she shouldn't underestimate Barrett. "That doesn't mean his threat isn't serious."

The scene in her office played out again in her mind. She couldn't forget that Jerome's animosity had stretched to Pete. "Jerome might bring you trouble. He believes in knocking down anyone or anything in his path."

"I've been knocked around a few times. I'm still standing."

She could melt so easily, Anne realized. Attraction was one thing, but he kept offering words of reassurance, a supporting arm, a sympathetic ear. "You'd be wise to walk away."

"I know what I'm walking into, but you didn't, did you?"

"No, I didn't." She hated the admission. The blue eyes on her were pushing her, prodding her to open her pain to him. "When I met Keith, I was working in the perfume department at one of his father's department stores and going to school for my degree. Keith was rich, sophisticated and persuasive. I was too unworldly for him, or I would have been more alert to how much he drank even then. After we were married, I realized the serious problem he had."

More memories crowded her mind, the good as well as the bad. Anne curled her fingers over the strap of her shoulder bag. If only she'd had something or someone to grip on to then. "I thought he'd change. He was always so contrite, so loving afterward. He always promised never again. But he couldn't break free of the problem."

"What did his father do?"

"Jerome wasn't aware of Keith's alcoholism, and Keith was afraid of his father's disapproval, always had been."

"And you never said anything to Jerome?"

The wind whirling around her, tossing her hair, she swiped strands away from her face. How could she explain? He'd been her husband, her family. "Never." She said the word with regret. Deep down, she'd always wonder if that was the biggest mistake she'd made.

"After I became pregnant, Keith's drinking became worse again. One night we had an argument. I couldn't take any more." She gazed at the crystal-white carpet beneath her feet, but all she saw was the darkness of those days when she'd worried about her husband, when she'd known she cared about him but no longer loved him. "I knew he was being unfaithful. I threatened to divorce him if he didn't get help."

Anne battled the tightness in her throat. "From what I learned later, Keith went home, told his father that I was threatening divorce, but never told him why. A good friend, a social worker used to dealing with similar problems, made me realize I was becoming a codependent and not helping Keith. Michael insisted that the tough-love theory was the only way to handle the situation."

A frown knitted his brow. "Michael's a friend?"

Anne nodded. "After talking to him, I'd hoped that even if my marriage couldn't be saved, Keith could be helped. I'd planned to tell Jerome and appeal to him to talk to Keith." Her voice softened to a whisper. "It was too late. Keith had been killed in an accident."

"It didn't happen too long ago, did it?"

"He died while I was pregnant."

His own arrogance taunted him. Almost flippantly he'd challenged her love for her husband. Insensitivity during that moment left a bitter taste in his mouth.

"I'm past the time of grieving," she answered truthfully. "The marriage was over before that happened."

"Didn't Barrett know that?"

Snow flurries rushed at her face, and cold penetrated her coat, skittering a chill through her again. "No, I don't think he wanted to see it. After Keith died, Jerome accused me of not being a good wife, of causing his son to run out after our argument. I tried to tell him that Keith had a problem for a long time. Jerome wouldn't listen or believe me."

Anne raked gloved fingers through her wind-tossed hair. "Keith's sister Christina could have told Jerome the truth. I knew she never would. I wasn't even married to Keith when she decided we needed to have a woman-to-woman talk. Bluntly, she told me I wasn't good enough for the family."

"If anything, I'd say it was the other way around." Pete clamped down an urge to draw her close and offer comfort. He'd only snatch the strength she was fighting for if he extended too much sympathy at the moment. But what right did Barrett, did anyone, have, to fill her with such fear? Helplessness filled him at the moment. As a lawyer, words flowed from his lips, but which ones would bridge the irrational ones of another man? He touched her arm and felt her shiver. Or was she trembling?

"Do you still want to go in?" she asked, with a thin smile.

When he saw that smile, he'd have agreed to anything. "Sure." Pete realized that Jerome Barrett would never understand her. A savage gust flapped at her coat as if sensing a frail opponent and trying to push her down, and though she hunched her shoulders against it, she kept her back straight. Always her steadiness, her resiliency, her determination to make the best of everything came through.

He followed her inside the store and eyed a lamp with a base that resembled an elephant. Oxidized, it looked like junk to him. Everything did in the room that was so cluttered, he had to turn sideways several times to inch his way to her.

"Isn't this lovely?" She spoke in the manner of someone who didn't have a care in the world. A tough lady, Pete thought with admiration. Another woman would be complaining, hanging on to a "woe is me" mood. He stared downward as her fingers grazed the wood of the Early American hutch. It looked old and scratched to him. The cliché about beauty being in the eye of the beholder came to mind. Frowning, he narrowed his eyes at a garish, gilded gold picture frame. "Junk," he mumbled.

His comment stirred her smile. Picking up a salt dish, she turned to show him. He was facing the window, frowning at a man and woman outside the store window. Though her encounter with the man had been brief, Anne recognized him. "Wasn't he at your house the other night?"

"His name is Marty." He gave a negligent shrug. "He has a nice wife."

Anne hadn't needed Pete to tell her that the man's wife wasn't the dark brunette who was nuzzling him at present. "Too bad," she murmured sadly.

Pete agreed, but unfortunately there was nothing he could do to stop a friend from making a big mistake.

They shuffled through one narrow aisle after another until they'd circled back to the front of the store.

"That's ugly," he said over her shoulder when she paused to study the frame of a mirror.

"Old," Anne countered.

Pete's gaze traveled the store. "Everything is old in here."

Laughing, Anne swung away toward the door.

Outside, the lunchtime crowd jostled against them. Taking a sidestep to dodge a woman lumbering with two shopping bags, Anne nearly collided with an eager beaver who'd just rushed out of the deli door.

In a proprietorial move, Pete yanked her close. The man braking inches from her was the youngest of the law recruits recently hired by the firm. "Do they still have you stuck in Acquisitions, Ned?"

"Eighteen hours a day."

Pete gave him a sympathetic grin as he relinquished his hold on Anne, but he hadn't been unaware at how perfectly her hip seemed to nestle against him. "Your lunch?" he asked, with a gesture toward the takeout bag in Ned's hand.

"Frank's."

Pete hid his displeasure. The kid was working his tail off to learn law, not to be someone's errand boy. "Want to work on mergers for a while with me?"

Ned's face noticeably brightened. "Yeah. That would be fantastic. Thanks." He started walking backward. "Thanks a lot."

Anne shot a smile up at Pete. "That was nice." She managed to sound steadier than she felt, but for a few brief moments when she'd been intimately pressed against him, an avalanche of emotions had rushed over her.

"He'll never get ahead the way he's going."

Anne doubted he knew what a phony he was. For a man who preferred a loner's existence, he willingly gave a great deal of himself to others. "Are you reluctant to admit you have a soft spot?"

"A soft spot?" Amused, he grinned as he urged her to resume walking.

"You do. You help others—Norma, Lolita, a young law recruit—me, and get nothing back," Anne insisted. "I bet you took in strays when you were a boy."

"No." Pete laughed. "No, I didn't take in strays. I was trying to watch out for myself and two brothers during those days. I didn't have time to worry about anything else."

She stared intensely at him. "But you are now."

"I wish I could play noble, but I'm not." He grinned in a way that warmed her. "I have a stack of work. I need his help."

"And Norma?" she challenged, not willing to let him brush away his caring nature so easily. "Why do you shovel snow for Norma?"

Stepping closer, he raised the collar of her coat to protect her neck. He thought he was being incredibly honest with her. For years, he'd concentrated on only one person—himself. A self-deprecating grin tugged up one corner of his mouth. "I have a thing for her chocolate-chip cookies."

His breath, a faint white mist in the frosty air, heated her face. "So ulterior motives abound?"

He stopped her with him and shifted so they stood only inches apart in a street bustling with other people. "Something like that."

"And what's your reason for helping me?"

He smiled in an amused way. She'd sparked something inside him he'd known maybe only once before in his life. Then, he'd been young and inexperienced. Until he'd met her, he'd always assumed he'd never feel it again. "You know why?"

A slow-moving shiver raced up her spine. The wind thrashed at them, but Anne barely noticed as her senses ganged up on her. The air carried the scent of winter, but she inhaled the woodsy one of his after-shave. The noise of traffic surrounded them, but the softness she'd heard in his voice wrapped around her. More from nervousness than humor, she laughed. "I thought you were a logical man," she said softly.

His eyes locked with hers. "Logic hasn't got a damn thing to do with this." With a fingertip, he traced the outline of her lips.

While the wail of the wind whistled in her ears, her heart thundered in her chest. As if she were under a spell, she remained still. He smiled then turned away, but distance didn't help. The warmth of his touch lingered on her lips.

Chapter Seven

In her whole life, Anne had never known any man who disrupted her life in such a way. Tense, she returned to her office. Whenever she'd been close to him, warmth had coiled in her belly, reminding her again of what she'd been avoiding since her marriage disintegrated. She was more than a mother; she was a woman with needs that weren't ready to be ignored.

By morning, she couldn't deny the underlying sensual storm that brewed ever since she'd met him. But she'd seen people lust and call it love. She didn't want to fall into the same trap.

Besides, love carried even more complications, especially love with a woman who was a mother. A man might love the woman but that didn't mean he would love her child. She knew that lots of other women willingly looked for a second time around. She wished them well, especially the ones with children.

But love wasn't a consideration between her and Pete. Plain and simple, desire crackled in the air between them. Her blouse hanging from her skirt, she flicked on the monitor that connected to the one in Rachel's room and started breakfast, then mechanically moved around the kitchen. She couldn't deny a longing to be with him, to feel his arms around her again. As a woman, she had needs. And as a mother, she was responsible not just for herself but also for someone else. Was there a middle ground where the two could blend?

She gave the clock one quick glance, the oatmeal another stir and hurried toward the bedroom for Rachel. Minutes later, she set Rachel in her high chair and propped cushions around her, then dashed to the stove. Luck was with her. When she shoved the spoon into the saucepan of oatmeal, it didn't scrape a coating at the bottom of the pan. "A few more seconds, honey," she assured Rachel.

Impatient, Rachel gurgled back with the threat of a cry.

Soothingly Anne crooned to her. Rushed as usual, Anne wiggled her toes into one pump and hunted through a drawer for one of Rachel's spoons. Not finding it, she washed the one in the sink and was heading for the table with the oatmeal when the telephone rang.

Anne set the bowl on the table and lifted Rachel. With her daughter in one arm, she limped to the

AN IMPORTANT MESSAGE
FROM THE EDITORS OF
SILHOUETTE®

Dear Reader,

Because you've chosen to read one of our
fine romance novels, we'd like to say
"thank you"! And, as a **special** way to
thank you, we've selected <u>four more</u> of the
books you love so well, **and** a Victorian
Picture Frame to send you absolutely *FREE!*

Please enjoy them with our compliments...

Dana Gavin Senior Editor,
Silhouette Special Edition

*P.S. And because we value our
customers, we've attached something
extra inside ...*

PEEL OFF SEAL AND
PLACE INSIDE

THE EDITOR'S "THANK YOU" FREE GIFTS INCLUDE:

▶ Four BRAND-NEW romance novels
▶ A pewter-finish Victorian picture frame

YES! I have placed my Editor's "thank you" seal in the space provided above. Please send me 4 free books and a Victorian picture frame. I understand I am under no obligation to purchase any books, as explained on the back and on the opposite page.

(U-SIL-SE-04/93) 235 CIS AH7N

NAME

ADDRESS   APT.

CITY   STATE   ZIP

Thank you!

DETACH AND MAIL CARD TODAY!

THE SILHOUETTE READER SERVICE™: HERE'S HOW IT WORKS

Accepting free books puts you under no obligation to buy anything. You may keep the books and gift and return the shipping statement marked ''cancel.'' If you do not cancel, about a month later we will send you 6 additional novels, and bill you just $2.71 each plus 25¢ delivery and applicable sales tax if any*. That's the complete price, and—compared to the cover price of $3.39 each—quite a bargain! You may cancel at any time, but if you choose to continue, every month we'll send you 6 more books, which you may either purchase at the discount price . . . or return at our expense and cancel your subscription.

* Terms and prices subject to change without notice. Sales tax applicable in N.Y.

If offer card is missing write to: Silhouette Reader Service, 3010 Walden Ave., P.O. Box 1867, Buffalo, NY 14269-1867

BUSINESS REPLY MAIL
FIRST CLASS MAIL   PERMIT NO. 717   BUFFALO, NY

POSTAGE WILL BE PAID BY ADDRESSEE

SILHOUETTE READER SERVICE
3010 WALDEN AVE
PO BOX 1867
BUFFALO NY 14240-9952

NO POSTAGE
NECESSARY
IF MAILED
IN THE
UNITED STATES

YOUR CHILD, MY CHILD

phone. "Hello," she said over Rachel vocalizing in her ear.

"She sounds hungry."

"Pete?" Anne did a double-take at the clock. "It's only six-thirty. Aren't you up early?"

He didn't miss the softer quality in her voice and smiled as he clicked open the ironing board. "I've been doing that lately." He snatched a wrinkled shirt from the kitchen chair and flicked on the iron. "See what a good influence you two were."

It was impossible not to be flattered that he'd gotten up at least an hour early to call her. Anne toed the other pump closer.

In the background, Pete heard Rachel verbalizing. He laughed with the realization that until he'd met Anne he'd never had to deal with a chaperon before while trying to charm a woman. "I'll make this quick." A smile filtered through his words. "Get a sitter, spiff up and tomorrow night I'll take you to someplace that will impress you."

For a second, she let the softness in his voice float over her. "Is that what you're trying to do? Impress me?" Like a contortionist, Anne twisted the telephone cord behind her and stretched it.

"You're wounding me." Pete maneuvered the iron around the shirt buttons. "You know I'm trying to."

Anne laughed and used the back of her heel to feel for the chair leg then plopped down to spoon oatmeal into Rachel's bowed mouth.

"Seven o'clock?"

They'd gone beyond the time when she could resist with a lame excuse, and she realized she really didn't want to. He'd made his feelings clear. He wasn't interested in any real involvement. Ground rules had been declared. If they both knew what they did and didn't want, then no one should get hurt. "I'll meet you at Norma's house."

"I'll pick you up."

Anne appealed to his logic. "I'd rather you didn't because I have to leave Rachel with Norma. It makes sense that I come to your house."

A faint frown furrowed his brow. It wasn't the way Pete would have chosen. "Okay, you win this one." Grinning, he started to set down the telephone.

"Pete?"

He yanked the receiver back to his ear. "Yeah?"

"Did you find one of Rachel's spoons?"

"Yeah, I did." He smiled slowly. "Stop by tonight. I'll be home."

"Maybe," she answered.

He dropped the receiver back in its cradle and laughed. Her "maybe" had sounded a lot like a "yes" to him.

With the pressed shirt hooked on a finger, in passing the cupboard, he grabbed a cookie for breakfast, then ambled toward the bedroom. Even when she'd thumbed her nose at him, he'd wanted her. Hell, he'd wanted her almost from their first meeting.

More than once he'd wondered what it was about her that appealed to him. Beauty was obvious. Spirit was more accurate. He admired her fighting spirit. He saw a delicate, beautiful woman who grasped at humor, kept tipping her chin up defiantly, kept meeting any challenge that came her way. None of that sounded romantic, but it was the truth. As much as he desired her, he also liked her.

At five that evening, Anne hurried into the house, a new dress for the following evening draped over her arm. Holiday glitz filled the racks at the store with a dazzling array of sequined gowns, but she'd chosen a burgundy dress, a simple, silk sheath with spaghetti straps and a matching jacket.

The plastic that covered it rustled as she dropped the garment onto a chair to answer the ringing telephone. Anxious about being home again after days away, she considered ignoring the ring for a full second. But she was one of those people who'd race from the opposite end of the house to answer the ring of a telephone.

Winded, she mumbled a hello.

Karen greeted her with a laugh. "Bad timing?"

"No. It's great to hear from you." With the telephone receiver wedged between her jaw and shoulder, she took a new bottle of nail polish from a bag and listened to Karen's sympathetic words to Anne's news about the furnace.

"This is terrible."

Anne uncapped the bottle of nail-polish remover. "I'm sorry to be the bearer of bad news."

"Oh, the furnace has been on the fritz since we turned it on. Phil and I even expected to wake up one morning in subzero temperature, but I feel so bad it happened when you were there. What are you doing? You needed a place where Jerome wouldn't look for you. It isn't good that you're home, is it?"

"Not really, but I couldn't stay at your home or Pete's any longer and—"

"Whoa! Back up," she broke in. "When did you stay at Pete's?"

Anne capsulized the events that had made her and Rachel guests of his. "I couldn't stay any longer," she repeated, then added, to divert Karen from making too much of it, "He makes terrible coffee."

Karen responded to her humor with a laugh. "Yes, but everything else is so right, just like I told you, isn't it?"

Anne couldn't argue.

Subtlety wasn't Karen's style. "O-kay," she said, stretching out the word. "What's going on? Did something happen?"

"Nothing."

"What happened?" she asked more excited. "He's called you?"

"Yes."

"You've dated?"

"Yes."

"Why am I pulling the words out of you?"

"He's not the kind of man who makes much room in his life for a woman, much less a woman with a child."

"Do you plan to marry him?"

"No," Anne said emphatically, not believing Karen would even think to ask the question. "I'm not planning to marry anyone. You know that."

"Then what is the problem? Be with him. Enjoy yourself."

Enjoy, Anne mused.

How easy Karen made that sound, she reflected, when she pulled her car in front of Norma's an hour later to pick up Rachel.

Slouched on the sofa, Pete munched on a taco, feeling annoyed for no good reason. Well, maybe one. After his phone call to Anne, he'd been certain she'd stop by. But the sound of his own wristwatch ticking by minutes bonged like Big Ben in his mind. He reminded himself he had no reason to be provoked. She hadn't promised. If he was disappointed, it was his own damn fault.

He was acting like a fool, but it was too late to pretend he could walk away. She wasn't like any other woman to him. He'd talked over morning coffee with her. He'd shared the pain of his childhood with her. He'd already known an intimacy with her unlike any he'd had with any other woman. And how often had he thought he was going mad because he couldn't stop thinking about her?

He ate the second taco he'd brought home with him and balled the wrapper. Two more sat in a bag on the kitchen table. He'd barely finished the two he'd had.

Frustrated, he charged to the living room window to see if her car was gone.

It wasn't. Through a blurry haze of snow, he could see her standing near the rear tire pumping a jack.

Pete released a lusty oath, snatched his jacket and stormed out the door. "You couldn't come to the door and ask for help?" he yelled over the wail of the wind as he stomped down the steps.

With a look over her shoulder, her hair flew across her face.

"Did you hear me?"

She took a breather from her battle with the lug nut. As he glared at her, her back straightened. Everyone in the neighborhood had probably heard him.

"What are you trying to prove? That you don't need anyone? Ever?"

"I've done this before," she returned irritably, not in the best humor herself at the moment. She strained to turn the second lug nut, wishing she could shoot whoever invented those air guns mechanics used that made it impossible for human strength to match.

Pete saw red when she leaned into the lug wrench. Standing beside her watching her struggle, he felt about as useful as the jilted boyfriend at his ex-lover's engagement party. "Get up."

Anne stilled and stared up at him. "I need to change this or I can't—"

"Get up!" His breath puffed on the freezing air. His eyes narrowed to dark slits. Wind whipped at his hair, tossing snow at him as he stood beneath the moon-light looking like some champion of a land. "You're not doing it while I'm here," he shouted at her.

Anne bent back to the task and clenched her teeth to budge the bolt. "Don't be dumb," she tossed back between puffs. "If you weren't here, I'd change it."

"Well, I *am* here." In a lightning-quick move, he grabbed her arm and yanked her to a stand, nearly unbalancing her. "Go in the house. I'll do it."

His manner, more than his offer made her bristle. Her face lifting, she met his eyes squarely. "Neanderthal tactics don't suit you."

Despite the mantle of night, he could see the fury sparkling in her dark eyes. He understood the warning but couldn't back off. He had an enormous desire to strangle some sense into her. "Just take Rachel inside where it's warm," he said with strained calm.

Furious, Anne turned away in a huff. If he wanted to play macho man so badly, then let him.

"There's dinner on the kitchen table," he called out between grunts while loosening the obstinate lug nut.

Cradling Rachel in the carrier, Anne paused in her steps up the walkway. It would serve him right if she devoured everything in sight. She set Rachel down in the living room and loosened her blankets. Not sure how long it would take him to change the tire, she eased her sleepy daughter's arms and legs out of the snowsuit and re-covered her with a blanket.

Still fuming at his caveman attitude, she stormed into the kitchen. Anne braked before the kitchen table. On a laugh, she fingered his dinner offer—two soggy-looking tacos. She wasn't *that* hungry.

Pete prepared for a battle when he entered the house several minutes later. In passing, he noticed Rachel was sleeping as if there was nothing wrong in the world.

Pete found her mother in the kitchen, Rachel's spoon in her hand. She didn't look as serene. Her face still flushed, her eyes glowed with emotion.

A cautious man by nature, he decided to give her a few more cooling-off minutes and crossed to the sink. Water rushed from the spigot, cutting into the silence that hung like a heavy curtain between them. He'd acted like an idiot. Frustration made idiots of men, he excused. He wanted to give more than she wanted to receive, and it angered him. He washed hands that felt numb from the cold then slowly turned to face her. "Okay." He planted his feet, steeling himself for words that would sweep her out of his life completely. "Yell."

Snow dusted his hair and shoulders. The color of a pomegranate, his face shone with moisture and his nose rivaled Rudolph's brilliant one. In Anne's mind, only an ungrateful fool wouldn't appreciate his freezing for her. "What should I yell about? You freezing so I could be warm?"

Baffled, Pete gave his head a shake. Why had he even tried to second-guess her? More than once, she'd puzzled and infuriated him. Constantly she drove him crazy because he wanted her so bad, he couldn't think straight.

He stepped closer, bridging the distance until only inches separated them. Just the sight of her made him ache. Unable to resist touching her, he let his fingertips play across the nape of her neck. "No tongue lashing about chauvinism?"

Anne laughed to relax herself. Nothing felt steady— not her breathing, her pulse or her heart. She stared into eyes darkening to the color of a stormy sky, eyes filled with desire's tenseness. "I might think of some choice words later." She wanted to sound in control, but her pulse mocked her, racing at an uneven pace. "For now. Thank you." She took a deep breath and glanced at the tacos. "You haven't finished..." She paused as he fingered the buttons on her coat. "Your dinner." Desire hummed through her. With one step back, she could stop this. But she didn't want to. "Aren't you hungry?"

Barely touching her, he slipped her coat off, first one shoulder and then the other. "For you," he murmured.

She braced herself for sensation as his arm slid around her back, but too many swarmed in on her at once. "This is—" She released a soft smoky laugh that was threaded with amusement and uncertainty and desire.

"I don't know what this is, either," he murmured as her scent filled him. "But running from it won't stop it."

Anne felt herself melting.

"I've known your kiss," he whispered against her cheek. "I've felt your arms around me." His mouth hovered near hers, the warmth of his breath mingling with her own. "That's what I'm sure of."

Sensations. Emotions. Desire. All that and more seemed to be consuming her even as she challenged him, even as she swayed closer. "Are you always so sure of yourself?"

"No. I only know I want you. Too much. Too damn much."

The pleasure of the moment swept through her. Her pulse thudding, her blood pounding, she framed his face with her hands and drew his mouth down to hers, yearning for what she'd denied wanting.

The memory of every other woman fled from his mind. He felt the craving, raging in him. He meant to be gentler. This woman deserved gentle. But as her mouth answered his, as her hands touched his back, as he buried his fingers in the softness of her hair and the silky strands tangled around his fingers, an aching need whipped through him. He couldn't remember it ever coming over him so swiftly. His mouth heating beneath the warmth of hers, he pressed himself into her softness, heard her soft moan.

There was nothing beyond this moment or this woman for him. There was a seductive tenderness weaving a web around them, and she was the spinner. She gave more than she knew, more than he'd been prepared for. He wasn't seventeen anymore, and his knees had never weakened from a kiss—never—until now.

Anne drew a long breath, feeling the need to fill her lungs, do something to relax the excitement suddenly pounding through her body. They both knew how far to let emotion take them. Eventually they'd go their separate ways. But tonight, did that have to matter? Tonight, couldn't she do as Karen had said? Enjoy, Anne reflected. Yes, she wanted to. She wanted to forget the trouble in her life for a little while. She wanted any moments she could have with him. "I do want you," she whispered, as a heat soared inside her.

Pete realized he'd needed those words from her. His fingers wound into her hair. His mouth captured hers again as if this were the only time he'd kiss her. She murmured something. He didn't need more words. The mouth on his, heating his, carried its own message. Most of his life, he'd controlled his emotions. There was no control now. His mouth clinging to hers, he gathered her in his arms to carry her to the bedroom.

In the moonlit room, they sank to the mattress. With her dark hair draped across his pillow, her pale skin, all the emotion he'd been holding back was unleashed. As he pushed aside her blouse, she sought the buckle on his belt. Pete felt no patience for either of them. Hands yanked at cloth, tugging it from each other. Even before the last wisp of silk whispered off her, his hands were roaming relentlessly.

With the tip of his tongue, he grazed skin that was delicate. Warm. Soft. Everything he'd imagined, more than he'd expected.

Passion clawing at him, he taunted. He pleased. His mouth lingered and persuaded until he heard her soft moan. Her excitement feeding him, he moved lower, his hand following curves. He touched again what he'd only allowed himself to imagine before. Madness made him want to rush, drag her against him and bury himself in her softness, but he heard her soft whimper, and he lingered, letting his lips and tongue tumble her over the first of many peaks.

Breathless, her heart thundering, Anne clutched at his arms. Through a cloud of sensation, she heard his harsh breaths, felt his need against her thigh, but he showed her a patience she hadn't expected. She'd seen him push and challenge. And yet, now he offered the sensuous caresses of a lover.

She tried to catch her breath, but with each moist flick of his tongue, her world rocked. She sank into a whirling abyss where a fire ignited. His touch no longer soothed and stroked but insisted until she was writhing beneath the slightest brush of a finger.

A wave of heat hurled her. She heard her raspy breaths blending with his, felt the urgency in his hands, the insistence in his mouth, and all that mattered was feeling him against her, in her. Flesh-to-flesh blending. "Please," she whispered, wrapping her legs around him, framing his face with her hands and urging his mouth to hers to speak a message she hadn't offered in a long time.

On a muffled moan, he buried his face in the curve of her neck. As he pressed down, she relinquished all that her heart could give. As he plunged, she welcomed him to her, letting her heat envelop him.

Breathless, she murmured his name, stroked his back, cupped his buttocks, strained against him and with him. Head back, she closed her eyes, whirled into another world. She gasped to keep pace with the inferno lifting her, lapping at her, then arched to meet and rock with him as the fire flared and burst through her. An explosion lit her mind, and the roar of the blaze resounded with a final message, a taunting message. In that instant between the madness of pleasurable torment and the fog of reality, she knew that no matter what happened between them, she'd never be able to forget him. Never, she thought briefly, before surrendering to the final wave of heat.

For a long moment she clung, waiting for her breathing to return to normal, waiting for no reason except that oneness with him seemed right. Why had she denied wanting this? Why had she tormented herself? She inhaled the scent of him, her fingers skimming over the sleekness of his shoulders and the bunching muscles in his back.

She listened to his breathing, which was no longer harsh or quick, and nuzzled her face deeper into the curve of his neck. Her mind warred with her body, urging her to leave. To stay would add another dimension to the moment. But right now she was too content to move. With the warmth of him around her, she didn't want to let the outside world in. She reminded herself they'd uttered no promises and no false words of love. Accepting with an open heart what they'd shared, she had one thought, only one thought. She wanted him again. "That was..." She smiled as he raised his head to look at her. "Wonderful."

Lazily with a possessive touch, Pete caressed flesh that carried the musky scent of passion. "No, better. Incredible," he whispered, shifting to ease his weight from her.

Anne held tight and drew him back to her to absorb the feel of him, smooth and hard against and in her for a little longer.

"I still owe you a night out," he murmured with husky softness.

"Tomorrow," she whispered, her hand gliding down and over his buttocks.

She didn't have to say more.

Chapter Eight

She was gone when Pete awoke the next morning. For some reason, he knew she would be, but he still felt disappointment. He'd wanted to awaken beside her, stare into her eyes, feel the heat of her against him.

In his wildest dreams, he hadn't imagined that loving her would be so consuming or that he'd tremble from it. Even now, her scent, her taste, her softness lingered in his memory.

As giving as she'd been, he'd never doubted that she was intent on keeping some distance between them. She still puzzled him, he realized. She was like a chameleon. Sometimes so serious and unyielding that he wanted to shake her. Sometimes filled with such youthful mischief and good humor that he forgot everything serious in his life. She was good for him. As good as he was for her.

He realized he had no choice except to take one moment at a time. But for the first time since he'd begun working at the law firm, as he sat behind his desk later that morning, he wanted to be somewhere else, anywhere else as long as it was with her.

Usually Anne would wish to be somewhere else other than wasting time waiting in a doctor's office, but she felt amazingly carefree during one of the most disturbing times in her life. She didn't even mind the hour wait in the pediatrician's office and then another two hours in line for a driver's license renewal. She daydreamed—something she rarely did. She remembered a night like she'd never known. She couldn't recall ever feeling this way, not even during blissful times with Keith. And then she'd been in love.

But what she had with Pete wasn't love. She wouldn't act foolish just because they'd shared a night of passion. They'd both received and gave. Passion carried no promises, fulfilled no dreams. She accepted mutual need as their binding force. That was a mature way of thinking.

She continued with the same reminder even when later she zipped her car into the restaurant parking lot to meet Linda for lunch.

Producing a quick smile, she joined Linda at the table. Knocked out from an immunization shot, Rachel snoozed in the carrier seat.

Linda wasted no time. Over an oversize platter of Oriental chicken salad, she prodded, "Are you going to keep me in suspense? All you told me on the phone earlier was that you'd seen him last night. How did the evening go?"

"Nice."

Rachel whimpered, snagging Anne's attention. As Anne curled Rachel's fingers around a set of colorful rings that never failed to fascinate her, she wondered what she could say to Linda. She was still surprised herself by the depth of emotion that Pete had aroused in her.

"Oh, so innocent."

Anne's smile widened at her friend's tease.

"Anne, it's all right to have fun again."

"You sound like Karen." Anne feigned a scowl that drew her friend's laughter. "Have you two been conspiring against me?"

"*With* you," Linda assured her.

Of course, they only wanted what they thought was best for her.

"We care about you. He does, too. I could tell," she added between bites of chicken. "When he came into the office, I could tell he wanted to take a poke at Jerome. I wish he had."

Anne laughed because the whole situation seemed so out of control.

"So the evening was romantic?"

"You're wonderful but definitely nosy."

"Just a little bit," she said in her own defense. "Aren't you going to answer my question?"

"It was romantic."

"Ah." Her hands came together in a clap. "So love is in the air."

No, Anne thought. It can't be love.

* * *

At seven that evening, Pete was as nervous as he'd been on his first-ever date, which seemed dumb. He'd already made love with her. Since that evening when she'd appeared on his doorstep, she'd been with him more than any other woman in the past year. They weren't strangers. They'd disclosed their pasts to each other. They'd shared private pain. Hell, they'd played house together—almost.

But when he opened the door for her minutes later, he felt the same sensations he'd known at sixteen when he'd worn his best jacket and had faced Cindy Johnson, a perky blonde in his history class, who'd played cat and mouse with him for a month. She'd dazzled him. Anne stunned him.

He'd expected to feel the punch in his gut that a man encountered when facing a beautiful woman. He didn't expect his knees to weaken. During time together when she'd worn sweatshirts and jeans, he'd begun to see more than her outer beauty. Now it slammed at him as if to call him a fool for forgetting what had attracted him to her in the first place.

"Is something wrong?" Anne stepped forward and placed the car seat on the carpet by the sofa. A sleeping Rachel never stirred.

"Everything is right. You look lovely."

She released a long, not too steady breath. "Thank you." She pirouetted, a touch self-conscious at his compliment. To some degree, she supposed it was natural to have "morning-after" nerves at their first meeting since last night.

As he smiled, he tugged her close. "Next time, don't slip away so quickly," he murmured against her hair.

Next time, she repeated to herself. Yes, there would be a next time. "I won't," she answered and knew she meant it. Drawing back, she outlined his lips with her fingertip. "I should take Rachel over to Norma's."

"There's no need."

His words were drowned out by stomping on the steps. "Well, here I am," Norma called out.

Anne darted a look from Pete to her. "You're going to sit for Rachel here?"

"Pete thought it would be better." Armed with a bag of potato chips and a liter of soda, she beamed and breezed past Anne. "That's fine with me. I like the big-screen television."

Anne wondered what else he had planned. In little ways, he took her breath away.

Resembling a medieval castle, the hotel catered to celebrities. Its restaurant was tucked between the huge marble lobby and its landscaped grounds. It was an "in" place for celebrities, a restaurant Keith's sister had raved about.

Seated at the table, Anne gazed out the wall of windows. In summer, a garden offered a profusion of blossoms and color. In winter, patrons viewed an unmarred carpet of white glistening beneath the moonlight. "It's really beautiful here."

"I like the view," Pete said softly.

She slanted a smile at him. When he wanted to charm, he did it well.

A well-known linebacker for the Denver Broncos and a 1940s film star in town to appear in a local play passed by. A buzz of excitement traveled with them.

"We're hobnobbing with celebrities," she whispered.

"Impressed?"

"Not with them." She laughed with a memory. "I gave up idol worshiping at thirteen."

He heard the lightness in her voice and smiled. "What traumatic event occurred?"

"Jeffrey Kellog kissed me." A giggle slipped out. "I was absolutely crazy about him. I decided then that live males were definitely better than any one on a stupid poster."

"Intelligent deduction," he returned, grinning.

"I thought so." She looked away as a feminine voice that sounded cultured and insisting called out his name.

Tall and leggy, a blonde glided up to their table.

Standing, Pete stood still as she rubbed her cheek against his.

"I haven't seen you in ages," she gushed.

Pete couldn't believe his luck. Never had he run into an old girlfriend while with another woman. "How are you, Geneva?"

"Married." She flashed a rock-size diamond at him and tugged the man behind her forward to introduce him. "You aren't yet?" Impertinently she swept an assessing gaze over Anne.

"Why would you think I might be?"

She arched a brow as if amused he'd asked that question. "I heard you might be the next partner at the law firm. Doesn't Amos Klein still believe marriage is man's destiny?''

''As adamantly as ever,'' Pete answered.

Her eyes strayed again to Anne. ''Well, it was nice seeing you again,'' she said as a goodbye. Hooking her arm with her husband's, she sauntered forward. A couple followed on her heels, but the woman stalled abruptly.

Almost in unison with Anne, Christina Barrett seemed to catch her breath.

Why was it whenever a person wasn't prepared for something, it happened? Anne reflected. Keith's sister hadn't changed. She was willowy like a ballerina. Miss Junior League was stamped on her. She was the last person Anne wanted to see, yet the one Anne knew she might need desperately to reason with Jerome.

Disdainful blue eyes flicked over Anne, then froze on Pete for a long second before she turned away. As her anger had rippled on the air to him, Pete had felt every protective instinct he possessed rising for Anne. ''Who the hell was that?''

''Christina Barrett, Jerome's daughter. Her venom is lethal.''

Pete frowned at the lousy luck for both of them. ''Are you wounded?''

Anne gave him a wry smile. ''No, but you should be stung.''

''Guess I chose the wrong restaurant.''

''No, it's lovely here.'' She sent him another smile to ease the frown wrinkling his brow. ''Do you come here often?'' Despite the question, her gaze shifted from him.

Over his shoulder, Pete traced her stare, wondering what else was going to go wrong. Just then, a giant of a man, wide and tall, with a grin as overabundant as his stature, was approaching their table.

''Pete, nice to see you again,'' he said, in a thick Southwestern twang, steps from the table. Decked out in a Western-style suit, he puffed a fat cigar between words. ''I contacted your lady friend.''

After the encounter with the gushy blonde, the last thing Anne wanted was to know more about his love life.

''She's quite a character, Pete. She made me sign a handwritten contract that I'd never renege on our agreement even after she saw the Pearly Gates.''

Curiosity ended Anne's fascination with the thin stem of her wineglass.

''It was a real experience, but we reached an agreement.'' Grinning broadly, the man's round cheeks bunched like a chipmunk's. ''I always thought of a woman named Lolita as long-legged, blond and sultry.''

''Fifty years ago, she might have been,'' Pete returned.

The man laughed robustly, turning heads in his direction. ''I think I was born a little late.'' He nodded his head at Anne. ''Sorry to interrupt you,'' he said, and walked away.

''He's a real character,'' Pete commented with a laugh.

Her interest snagged, Anne waited only until he sat again. "What happened with Lolita?"

"The city okayed her farm as a bonafide animal adoption shelter. Cal Perkins," he said with a gesture toward the man exiting the restaurant, "is an animal activist with money. He'll provide funds for kennels. She manages it. She had the room for it, a couple of acres. So she keeps and feeds the strays until they're adopted."

"What if they aren't?"

Pete wasn't surprised by her question. Sensitive, she'd see the flaw in his perfect plan. "Rest easy. If they don't, then she and the animals grow old together."

A smile sprang to her face. "Sounds perfect."

"Nothing ever is, but I believe any plan is better than giving up."

Anne returned his smile. She didn't understand him, she realized. In a short period of time, she'd witnessed a man of great emotion with an enormous capacity for caring about others, but for some unexplainable reason, he'd convinced himself he was a solitary man. Conveniently he seemed to forget the people he did help.

"Why so quiet?"

Anne laughed. "A better question is, why are you smiling at your salad?"

The flame of a candle shifted light and shadows across her face, bestowing him with only a taunting picture of her. "I was thinking how long it's taken me to get here with you."

"You're a very persistent man." Incredibly she realized her pulse thudded harder just from his warm stare. "Why didn't you take no for an answer?"

He sipped his wine. It carried a rich, sweet flavor that lingered on his tongue, but all he could think about was a different taste, one he'd been hungering for all night. "We'd shared too much for me to walk away."

She hunched forward to whisper across the candle-lit table. "Are you talking about last night?"

"Even before that." He took her hand. "We'd already awakened together."

Anne laughed softly. "That's stretching the truth, Counselor."

"And we've sung in the same shower."

With the stroke of his thumb at her wrist, her hand tingled. "I don't sing in the shower."

"I heard you singing a walloping rendition of 'Wind Beneath My Wings.'"

Anne cracked a smile. "It's better than 'When the Saints Go Marching In.'"

"And we'd shared the same bed," he said softly. "Even when you were gone, your scent was with me." Beneath his fingers, he felt her pulse scramble. "I'd say that we were very intimate even before last night."

Candlelight accented the hard angles of his face as he shifted to lean closer. Anne bowed her head and stared at his fingers linked with hers. Was a bond forming? she wondered, a touch uneasy at the thought.

*   *   *

"Not a peep out of her," Norma said between yawns when Anne and Pete entered the house.

Anne wasn't surprised. She'd been fortunate to have what people termed a "good baby." Rachel was rarely cranky, usually smiling when people talked to her.

"I'm going to walk Norma home," Pete called out.

Anne checked on Rachel, but instead of disturbing her, she strolled toward the kitchen to make coffee. A dozen excuses for waiting popped into her mind, like politeness for a wonderful evening or sympathy for Pete's taste buds. Only one carried the truth. She wanted to be with him anytime she could.

The coffee was perking by the time Pete returned.

Stockinged feet tucked under her, she sat on the sofa, staring at the television. "Caught me." She turned a smile up to him. "I never miss a Spencer Tracy and Katharine Hepburn movie."

"My luck it's on tonight," Pete said, sitting and draping an arm behind her on the sofa.

As his mouth brushed her ear, she laughed. "Of course I'd watch any of the old movies."

His whisper fanned the curve of her neck. "The sign of a romantic at heart."

"Are you?"

He caught a handful of her hair and threaded fingers through it. Like a seductive glove, raven strands tumbled over his hand. Soft, scented, they lured him to bury his face in them. "I have my moments."

"Yes, you do," she said with a soft laugh.

He'd never expected this intensity, this drive for any woman. Other men had talked about it. He'd thought them fools—until now. "I've been thinking."

She'd been trying not to. She pressed her body against him, lured by his soft gentle kisses. "A dangerous thing, sometimes."

"It's one thing to let you drive here, but it's nearly midnight now," he said, huskier than usual.

As he toyed with a strap of her dress, he brushed his lips across her collarbone. "And?" she asked a touch breathlessly.

"Wouldn't be safe..." He paused, distracted by her fingers on his chest, playing with a shirt button.

"I should stay," she whispered, while one by one the buttons opened beneath her fingers.

The impatience in her voice was like an echo in his mind. Pete released a muffled laugh. "Yes, stay," he murmured, then fastened his mouth over hers.

In a jumble of sheets, his legs tangled, Pete awoke with a start, ready to fight. Only a second passed. Beside him, he felt Anne's breathing, slow and even. "You awake?" he mumbled against her temple.

Squinting against the sunlight streaming in from the bedroom window, Anne burrowed herself deeper under the covers. She'd slept through the night, never aware she wasn't alone or somewhere other than in her own bed. Yawning, she snuggled closer to him, not ready yet to talk. In answer, she brushed her mouth across his chest.

"Guess so," he said quietly on a soft chuckle.

Eyes closed, she stretched beside him, pushing her length against him and draped a leg over his. "Want coffee?"

Against his rib, he felt the steady beat of her heart. Last night, it had raced, thundering against him, matching his. "Well, that wasn't the first thought in my mind."

A smile curled her lips. "I have to get up. Almost time for the morning siren."

"But she isn't awake yet." Feather-light, he skimmed a hand over the sharp point of her hip.

Anne slitted her eyes to gaze up at him. Blue eyes sparkling with devilment met hers. He was like an addiction, a wonderful one that each day intensified her craving for more.

"I have an idea." He tucked strands of her hair behind her ear so he could nibble at it.

She managed a whispery laugh as his hand slipped between her thighs. "I know."

Rachel gave them only enough time to draw several normal breaths. As she began her serenade, Anne dashed from the bed. Dark hair flying, she offered Pete a delectable view of her backside before she slipped on one of his shirts. Slim, small-boned, she looked delicate and pale beneath the morning light. He smiled, almost amazed at the strength he'd felt in her slender thighs when they'd gripped him to her.

A contentment he hadn't believed existed filled him. He'd always been so sure of what he did and didn't want. Suddenly he wasn't sure of anything except a need to be with her.

Beneath him, the sheet felt cool where she'd been, but her fragrance lingered. Reluctantly he eased himself from the bed, and in slow motion he dragged on jeans and yanked a polo shirt over his head. Barefoot, he padded to the front door, retrieved the morning newspaper, then headed for the kitchen.

The music of Garth Brooks filled the room. Anne had chosen a soft ballad that Pete noted seemed to please Rachel. She babbled along with the singer, more patient than usual for her bottle.

Briefly he recalled more leisurely mornings. Yet, these abrupt awakenings were becoming more familiar quickly. "Are you going to be late for work?" he asked, while pouring coffee.

Patiently Anne waited for her daughter's bowed mouth to close around the nipple of the bottle. "Two days a week I go in late."

Distracted, Rachel's eyes followed Pete.

"Would you please sit down or she'll never stop watching you?"

He smiled, liking the way her hair looked, tousled from sleep and his hands. "I'm down." He dropped to the closest chair. "So what are you having for breakfast?"

"I don't want breakfast."

"Not even pancakes." At the shake of her head, he tried again. "French toast?"

"Are you trying to convert me into a breakfast eater or finagle me into cooking for you?"

Sitting back in the chair, he rested his heel on his denim thigh and sent her an offended look. "Would I do that?"

Exaggeratedly she sighed, holding back a smile. Had she ever stopped wanting this part of the dream? After her marriage had ended, she'd still longed for someone to talk to in the morning, someone to share breakfast with, someone who'd look at her with smiling affection.

"I'm only thinking of your welfare," he said, cutting into her thoughts. "And Rachel's. You have to set a good example."

Anne laughed at the ridiculousness of his comment. "At the moment, Rachel doesn't need any persuading. She loves food at any time."

He rolled the rubber band off the newspaper. "But some day she'll emulate you. She'll want to be like her beautiful mother and then she'll see that you don't eat breakfast and—"

Anne raised a hand in surrender. "All right. Do you want French toast?"

"I thought you'd never ask."

"I don't understand that you don't cook. You're a bachelor." She expressed her puzzlement. "When you were younger, didn't you cook for your brothers?"

"All the time and as little as possible." Skimming the front page of the newspaper, he ran fingers across the stubble on his jaw. "Jimmy always wanted hot dogs."

"The youngest?" Anne ventured, ambling to the stove for her daughter's cereal.

Pete nodded. "And David liked everything."

Anne squinted against the morning sunlight to see his expression. "What did you make for them?"

Humor danced in his eyes. "Cold bean sand-wiches."

Aware she was touching a sensitive topic, she mea-sured her next words before speaking, "What are they doing now?"

"David owns a small landscaping company. And Jimmy works with computers."

Not deaf to the concern that had crept into his voice, she was quick to point out, "Neither of them did badly."

"Guess not." He was amazed they'd all weathered some difficult years well. Vivid memories of anger at his father, of guilt that he couldn't have done more for his brothers lingered, but the bitterness seemed to have vanished. With unseeing eyes, he stared at the news-paper. "I was a lousy cook." A wry, sad smile touched his lips. "Poor kids."

You, too, Anne thought, staring at his profile as he eased off the chair. She saw a man's determination in the firm set of his strong jaw, but for a fleeting sec-ond, she'd heard a hint of a boy's sadness and vulner-ability.

One by one, he opened and closed cabinet doors. "Little has changed. There are still no groceries in the house."

Anne caught his stab at humor. "How often do you go to the grocery store, Counselor?" she teased, to help him lighten his mood.

"Often."

"How often?"

Squinting, he stared up at the ceiling as if searching it for an answer.

"Admit it," she said, laughingly. "You survive on greasy hamburgers and chocolate cookies from the convenience store."

"Guilty." He didn't look one bit repentant.

Snowflakes were fluttering in the air by the time they returned from the grocery store. Besides eggs and bread, the grocery bag overflowed with a bag of tortilla chips, a package of chocolate sandwich cookies and a box of something called Rainbow Pops that Pete declared was "food for the soul." Anne left him to unpack his goodies and disappeared into the bedroom to change Rachel's diaper.

In between unpacking a grocery bag, Pete called his office to convey a simple message to his secretary.

She offered a greeting and a message of her own.

Pete dropped the loaf of bread back in the bag, the authoritative voice of Amos Klein demanding his full attention.

"Yes, personal business. Unexpected," Pete said in response to Klein's questioning about his coming in late. Distractedly he followed Anne's easy, fluid stride across the room.

"Your secretary told me you'd be in later. That's fine. But I couldn't wait to talk to you. My wife will be calling me at noon. If you had a wife you'd understand that when they're planning a party, they become Napoleonic," he said, with a trace of laughter. "You will be coming, I assume."

Forgetfulness rarely entered his life. When it became cluttered, he'd relied on lists and an appointment book. The problem was he'd forgotten to check the appointment book. Hell, other than Anne, everything had slipped his mind lately, including Klein's birthday bash. "Yes, sir, I'll be there."

"Fine. And will you be bringing someone?"

A good question, Pete mused. "I intend to."

"That's excellent. I'll look forward to meeting her."

Pete hooked the receiver back in the cradle. Now, all he had to do was convince Anne to go with him. A man who'd learned patience, he decided to ease into a discussion about the party. "Okay, so what's the first step in making French toast?"

More interested in the voice behind her than the spoon in Anne's hand, Rachel looked up and got a cheekful of beets.

Anne dabbed a wet cloth at her daughter's face. "You're going to cook?"

A hand over the top of the refrigerator door, he feigned a scowl. "I'm capable of starting it. Now, what do I need?"

She shot a quick grin at him. "Eggs." As he buried his head in the refrigerator, Anne perused his backside in the snug jeans. Who said women didn't ogle? Of course, they did. Discreetly.

"That was the boss on the phone," he began as absently as he could manage. "How would you like to go to a party Saturday evening? A birthday party for the senior partner."

Anne nearly fed Rachel's cheek again. While her future bordered on tumultuous, his was nearly settled. He didn't need her in his professional life, too, complicating it. "It isn't sensible."

"I agree," he said, deliberately twisting her words. "The candles on the cake will look like an inferno. And he doesn't have the air power to blow them all out."

Anne sent him an impatient look. "Things are getting confusing."

"Yeah." Denseness wasn't his style, but he thought the moment called for extreme measures. "What do I do with the eggs?" He palmed one in each hand.

"You need a bowl." Rachel bubbled the beets out of her mouth. From behind her, Anne heard him opening and closing cupboards.

"Got one," he said, sounding jubilant. "Now what?"

"Crack them in it."

Pete hit one on the edge of the bowl. Wincing, he released a lusty expletive as eggshells fell into the yellow liquid.

"Pete, listen..." Sidetracked, Anne didn't notice Rachel rejecting another spoonful. "About this party. I'm not the right type of woman for you to take to it."

"Right type?"

"Oh, don't play dumb," she said. But she was more annoyed with herself than him. A little voice inside was nagging at her with girlish notions of romance and someone special. "I'm sure you usually date beautiful, very sophisticated women."

Pete recalled the way she looked late at night—sleepy, her hair brushed and loose. He couldn't remember any woman ever looking more beautiful to him.

"I'm right. You are used to a different kind of woman. Beautiful and—"

He piped in, "And one who likes plays and museums."

Her brows veed. "Museums?"

He couldn't help smiling because she looked so serious, so damn cute. He gave into the teasing mood slipping over him. "Museums," he repeated.

"I've been through your house." She tilted her head and saw a mischievous grin tugging at the corners of his lips. It was a look he was stingy with, one that revealed a carefree manner lurking beneath his serious demeanor. "I saw not one—not two—but *three* baseball bats in your kitchen closet. You only need one for a burglar. Remember? When was the last time you went to any museum except the Baseball Hall of Fame?"

He laughed at the accuracy of her deductive powers. "Okay, you caught me. I get used to saying what's expected of me."

"See there. I'm right about being the wrong type for you. I rarely say what's expected of me."

"Honesty is a nice change of pace."

"I view it more as a tendency to stick my foot in my mouth."

Stubbornness taking root, he appealed to her softer nature. "Why don't we call this a favor for a favor?"

He'd done more than his share for her, Anne reflected but tried again. "I thought you were a sensible man."

"I am." Her comment was an understatement. "A sensible man reacts in a logical way to a situation.

What do I do with the eggs now?'' he asked, concentrating on scooping out the last bit of eggshell.

''Whip them.''

''What's the object?''

Of course, Anne mused. He'd want to have a plan. He'd made plans for himself most of his life. She and Rachel were probably the first deviation he'd had from his plans in years. ''You'll dip the bread into the egg batter. You'll need a plate for that.''

''Sounds simple enough.''

Pete wasn't paying attention to her common sense and Rachel was less than enthusiastic about lunch. Faced with two stubborn people this morning, Anne gave up.

At the final scrap of the spoon, Pete looked up from dipping a slice of bread into egg batter. ''Am I doing this right?''

You do everything right, she mused. That's what's wrong. ''You're becoming a culinary master.''

He looked unconvinced.

Anne joined him at the counter and set a frying pan on the burner. ''But I'll cook.''

''You're damaging my ego with that lack of confidence.''

''Oh, I have...'' A tease riding her tongue, Anne turned her face up to him.

His mouth stifled her words.

''Sneaky,'' she mumbled against his lips.

''I take advantage of every opportunity.''

''I thought you were hungry.''

His laugh drifted over her. ''Starving.''

Chapter Nine

Anne spent the afternoon and early evening trying to track down a special order at the store. Fortunately, she didn't have to drive to Norma's for Rachel. Because she was visiting her mother in a suburb near Norma's, Linda had volunteered for the job. During a coffee break, Anne telephoned Norma and explained who would pick up Rachel. In a way, she was glad she could avoid the trip, worried that she might run into Jerome's private investigator. Since he wouldn't be looking for Linda's car, she could come and go without being noticed if he was there.

The telephone receiver in her hand, Anne started to call the vendor about the missing order. Briefly she considered phoning Pete to tell him that she wouldn't be coming for Rachel. Her own mind ridiculed her before she'd punched out even one number. Just because they'd spent a few nights together didn't mean he wanted to know her every move. They each had their own lives. They weren't joined at the hip. He probably wasn't even home.

With every slam of a car door, Pete whipped toward the window to see if Anne had come to pick up Rachel. By nine o'clock, she still hadn't showed.

A foul mood descending on him, he cautioned himself to stop acting like a damn fool. Hadn't he vowed never to let any woman do that to him? Hadn't he seen his father fall apart after his mother died because he'd loved her too much? But he wanted more than moments in bed with Anne. Though he knew the danger in such thinking, he didn't allow himself to overanalyze what he felt for her.

At nine-thirty, with an evening's worth of work spread out on his sofa, he still felt restless. Already he'd rowed for twenty minutes and had taken a cold shower.

Frustration sent him into the kitchen. Cupboards yielded nothing. Snatching up his jacket, he strode toward the door, visions of burgers loaded with onions flashing in his head.

As he hit the threshold, Pete heard voices that stilled him. A biting wind whipped at his jacket, sending a shiver through him and urged him to dash to his car or step back inside the house. Instead, he planted his feet and craned his neck to see Norma's front walkway.

Hunched over to battle the chill, Norma retreated several steps from the man talking to her, the wind carrying her scratchy voice to Pete. "I don't know an Anne LeClare."

Protective instincts not only for Anne but also for Norma descended on Pete as he heard the man's angry response. "Don't play games with me. I know she's been at the Winslows. I checked her home last night. She wasn't there, so she has to be here."

Norma didn't quake. "You got a problem—it's yours, not mine," she snapped and scowled after him.

Jerome never looked back.

Pete waited, expecting at any moment that Jerome would storm toward him. But the car pulled away. "Norma?" Pete crossed the snowy lawn.

She whirled around, her brows bunched, a threatening look pinching her face with a network of lines. "He's her trouble, isn't he?"

"He's the one."

"I don't know what he wants from her, but I wouldn't help him cross the street."

Pete nodded agreeably. "When did Anne pick up Rachel today?"

She looked off toward the other side of the street as if contemplating. "Hmm, it must have been around four o'clock. But she didn't. Her friend did." Again, a thoughtful look settled on her face. "A woman named...named Linda. She said that Anne was working very late."

With a shake of his head over the hours he'd waited, Pete swung away. Pretending he was playing knight to a damsel in distress screamed false in his mind. He slid into his car and switched on the ignition. Emotion governed his action. He'd be damned if he'd let Jerome hurt her again.

Though the drive to Linda's had been shorter, exhaustion weighed Anne down by the time she'd driven home and had settled Rachel in bed. The day had seemed miserably long and stressful at work. And all she wanted to do now was relax.

She dropped to the sofa and reached for the television program guide. The side of her hand brushed against the telephone. Despite the self-imposed lecture she'd given herself earlier, she still wanted to call Pete. Emotion churned up inside her, making her almost ache for something as simple as the sound of his voice. That wasn't the way she was supposed to feel. She expected closeness, warmth, affection but not this need.

Disgusted, she vented her irritation with herself on the television and switched twice through channels quickly before settling on a talk show. The host's jokes were dying on the air.

Anne nudged herself from the sofa and poked at the off knob. She was midway across the room when the doorbell buzzed. With a quick about-face, she thought of Pete, hoped for Pete. Her fingers were curled around the doorknob before another thought hit her. What if it was Jerome?

Her first instinct was to gather Rachel in her arms. She even went so far as to whip around, but reasoning took control. What would she do then? she challenged herself. Hide? With a calming breath, she flung open the door and nearly swayed with relief into Pete.

Scaring her had been the last thing he wanted to do. He stalled, hating to tell her about Jerome, hating to see her smile fade as he knew it would.

"I didn't expect to see you this evening."

"Expect and want are two different things," he said, a touch annoyed she was playing it cool and impersonal. There was nothing impersonal about what he'd been feeling all day for her. "Did you *want* to see me?"

"Want?"

"A simple question."

"Yes, I wanted to see you," she said, unable to pretend differently. "Yearned."

"Come here," he said on a laugh and dragged her close. He felt her smile against his cheek and realized he needed these few seconds with her before he swept fear back into her life.

Gently, softly, he kissed her. Anne had prepared for passion. Instead, there was affection in his kiss and something disturbingly close to reassurance in his embrace. Running her hands up his back, she was stunned that this was what she'd been missing all day. Like it or not, she'd missed him. Her hand gripping his, she drew him into the house with her.

Pete followed her into the room with its pale blue sofas and cherrywood furniture. The first time he'd entered it, he'd felt its welcoming warmth. A collection of Waterford crystal gleamed behind the glass doors of a rosewood cabinet and propped against the side of an upholstered chair was a guitar.

"Want coffee?" she asked, with a smile, over her shoulder.

"Anne."

Her steps faltering, she copied his frown. "What's wrong?"

He drew a hard breath. Stalling wouldn't make a problem go away, he reminded himself. "I had to come. Jerome's looking for you."

She whipped around to face him squarely. "What?"

"He came by the house and was questioning Norma."

A trace of panic edged her voice. "What did Norma say?"

When he finished relaying the conversation between Norma and Jerome, concern clouded her eyes. "Bless her," Anne said quietly.

"She's pretty sharp. But she put him off only for a little while. He'll realize soon that you probably came back here. He's sure to come looking for you."

"I thought he'd be here by now. Obviously his private investigator isn't too bright."

In amazement, he caught her attempt at humor. "He's kept a surveillance on the Winslows' house."

But for how long? Anne wondered. Tension rippled through her body, tightening the back of her neck and her shoulders. "I'm not running again."

"That's brave. And if you insist on it, I'll battle right alongside you."

He would, she realized. He wouldn't back down from anyone or anything. This man with his practical mind, his ambition, his tenacity was as formidable an opponent as Jerome could be. But she never allowed herself to forget that this was her battle, not his.

"Let's use some common sense."

Her chin came up before she wheeled away. "Are you saying I lack it?"

"No, I'm not saying anything like that."

Her back to him, she stood by the window and peered into the darkness. Was Jerome or his private investigator already out there?

"Listen to me." He moved close behind her and cupped her shoulders. "Sometimes you have to take cover for your own sake. This is one of those times. Until you can talk some sense into him or get the police involved, you need to show caution. I don't want to see you lose Rachel."

Anne whirled around.

She looked paler to him. Hadn't he wanted to protect her from this? And he'd known he couldn't. "You told me that he threatened to take her. Don't give him the chance." He took her hand in his. "Now, tell me what you need to take with you?"

"Take with me?" She pressed fingertips to the dull throb at her temple. "Where?"

"My place."

Anne shook her head wildly. "He knows I'm there," she reminded him.

"No, he doesn't. He expects you to hide out at Karen's or here." He smiled wryly. "In fact, he came here last night."

"Last night? Last night I was—"

"With me."

She released a mirthless laugh at the complexity of the moment. "So I hide out at your home?"

"Do you have a better answer? You sure as hell can't stay here and do nothing."

The same conclusion had already entered her mind. She agonized, aware control of her life was slipping through her fingers. "I'm not running from him. I'm not going to let him turn my life topsy-turvy. I'll go to the police."

Pete knew what they'd say. She was wasting her time, but he didn't argue. "Okay." He grabbed her coat from the nearby chair. "Bundle up Rachel. I'll drive you to the police station."

Despite her stellar performance of strength, weariness filled Anne. In the bedroom, she bent over Rachel and bundled her into a snowsuit and a blanket. "I hope your mommy knows what she's doing," she whispered.

Rachel gurgled gleefully.

Standing in the doorway, Pete silently cursed the man she'd married, and every man who'd ever let her down. He backed away quietly, not wanting her to know he'd heard and carted out Rachel's high chair and Portacrib to his car.

Minutes passed before Anne rejoined him in the living room. She moved ahead of him out the door. Only one step was taken. Her hands clutched Rachel tighter as she stared at the blue sedan parked across the street.

"Don't panic," Pete said close to her ear.

Anne pressed her lips to Rachel's forehead. Easier said than done. If she had to, she'd claw anyone who tried to take her daughter. She cuddled a sleepy Rachel closer to her breasts, then twisted around to return to the safety of her house.

Blocking her, Pete gripped her upper arms.

"What is the matter with you?" Anne jerked free of his hands. "Let me go back in."

"No, that's not the answer. He'll come here, Anne."

"I can't—"

"Quiet," he whispered, his face only inches from hers. "Here's the plan. Go to your car. I'll go to mine. Meet you at the police station."

"He'll follow me," she murmured, not seeing any success in his plan.

"Sort of," he answered. Pete prayed his own arrogance didn't smack him down. "Trust me."

The last time she'd offered such total trust to a man, he'd flung it aside without hesitation. But this wasn't that man, she reminded herself.

"Go," he urged. Pete waited until she'd slid into her car, then dashed to his. Some strategies played well only in the mind. He hoped this wasn't one of those times. Using his car as a buffer between Anne's and the sedan made sense to him.

On the street slick with ice and bordered by huge drifts of snow, the sedan was stuck behind him. When he'd had enough of Pete's snail's pace, the idiot U-turned. By then, Anne's car had disappeared from sight. Relieved, Pete gave himself a mental pat on his back.

Five minutes later, he strolled into the police station.

He didn't need to know what Anne had learned. He found her sitting ramrod straight on a chair across the desk from a rotund man with white hair. The nameplate on his desk stated Detective Ray Henderson. He looked more inclined to play Santa Claus every Christmas than to chase criminals. As he frowned, a bushy white mustache twitched. "There's nothing we can do."

"Have you been listening?" Anne caught her own voice raising and softened it. "This man is threatening to take my child. Since when isn't a kidnapping threat taken seriously?"

"Did anyone else hear Mr. Barrett make that threat?"

Her stomach knotting, Anne shook her head.

"So we only have your word that he did."

"I wouldn't lie about something like this," Anne flared.

"People do lie." The detective shimmied his chair closer to his desk and sent Anne what she deemed was an apologetic smile. "I can tell you're scared. But our hands are tied." He set a meaty palm on a stack of papers and leaned toward her. "All we have is your word that Jerome Barrett is doing anything. Now, if this guy that you claim is following you, if he does anything, you know, makes a threat—well, then—"

"Never mind," Anne said with as much calm as she could muster. "The bottom line is I can't get a restraining order."

"We can't do anything without proof."

"So what is the answer?" Anne asked. "We wait until he does kidnap Rachel?"

"I'm sorry." The detective sounded genuine. "If the next time, someone is around, and they hear him make the threat—"

Anne bolted to a stand before he could finish. Nervously she gripped Rachel closer. She wished she hadn't come, as discussion about Jerome made his threat seem more vivid in her mind.

"My suggestion would be that you stay with friends. That way, someone would be with you at all times. It's a way of protecting yourself if he's serious about that threat."

"Now, do you believe I'm right?" Pete asked when they were strolling down the hall toward the exit.

Anne looked past him to the dingy pea-green wall and a bulletin board of Wanted posters. As they'd walked from the detective's office, their heels had clicked in unison on the tile floor. It seemed to emphasize what she was most afraid to believe. She wasn't alone.

For so long, she'd wanted someone special, someone who would share her dreams, her troubles. Now she had someone shouldering some of her problems and that scared her more than being alone.

Reaching around her for the door handle, Pete trapped her between the door and himself. "I never took you to be a stupid woman. Don't be one now, or you could lose your daughter."

Close to crumbling, Anne snatched at anger to maintain control. "Never!"

"I'm your best bet," he said softly, regretting that he'd taken a poke at what he knew was her most vulnerable spot.

As if giving her agreement, Rachel squealed between them and jabbed a finger at his mouth.

"She agrees." He draped an arm around Anne's shoulders and snuggled them both close to him. "You're outvoted. The safest place is my house."

Was it really? Anne wondered. Physically she and Rachel would be safer, but at what cost to her heart?

While Pete parked her car in his garage, Anne considered what few options she had and went to the telephone to place a call. Spooning coffee grounds into the basket of the brewer, she waited for the sound of a familiar male voice. "Michael," she said, in response to his greeting.

At the back door, all Pete heard was the man's name. He couldn't say what he felt at the moment besides confusion. He prided himself on being reasonable, a man with an inordinate amount of good sense. Yet his ears were humming and his blood was warming with jealousy. She'd told him the man was only a friend. Dammit, wasn't he more than that? Why call someone else when he was near?

Leaning back against the refrigerator, he reasoned with himself. He had no rights with this woman. He couldn't make any demands. She didn't want them. In the past, that had always been the way he'd operated. So why was he feeling differently this time? Why in the hell was jealousy as close to erupting as the next breath?

As she finished the call, her hand trembled when she pushed at the button on the coffee brewer. "I called Michael for help several days ago."

Pete faced himself honestly. It wasn't jealousy he'd been feeling. He flipped a chair around and away from the table to straddle it. That she'd relied on someone else had surfaced something undeniably close to hurt.

"I thought a professional, someone who dealt with others' problems, might be able to reason with Jerome. Michael said Jerome didn't believe him, either."

"Why would he think this guy—Michael—was lying about everything?"

Anne rolled one shoulder to loosen tight muscles. "He thinks Michael was my lover and would lie for me."

Tense, Pete stared at the floor. Anger thrashed within him, anger with himself more than her. Pride be damned, he told himself. What she didn't need was more problems. At the scrape of the chair legs when he arose, she jerked to attention. He'd seen her uptight often. He'd seen an array of moods. Each of them had fascinated him. This one always bothered him. "What's the next step?"

Of course he'd believe that there had to be more she could do. Because she needed it, Anne seized his encouragement like a lifeline. "Christina," she answered. Keith's sister might be her last hope at penetrating the wall of anger and hurt Jerome had erected.

"The lady with the venom?"

Anne laughed, then wished she hadn't. With the release of one emotion, another snuck up on her. Tears streaked her cheeks before she could stop them. "This is so dumb." She started to turn away and found her face suddenly pressed against his shoulder.

"It's not dumb," he soothed, stroking her hair.

Emotions too strong to resist pulled at her. With them came a sweet pang of longing for the gentleness of his strength. In his embrace, she almost believed everything would be all right. "Pete, you know I don't expect—"

"Shh," he said against her hair. He didn't want to hear what she'd planned to say. He knew she didn't want to get involved. He knew she'd had one failed marriage. He'd never planned to ask her for anything, but he suddenly wanted one thing. He wanted to forget everything either of them had said before.

Tenderly, in a way she was becoming familiar with, he framed her face with his hands and forced her eyes to meet his.

"I don't know where this is going any more than you do. But you need me. Stop fighting that." He pressed his lips against her cheek. "Because I'm not going away."

Chapter Ten

Outside the window of Pete's office, morning clouds crowded the sky. Impatiently he checked the clock on his desk. He thought the hands weren't moving. Time was dragging, and he had no excuse for his discontent except that he missed Anne.

By four-thirty that afternoon, he headed for the elevator with a briefcase heavy with work he hadn't finished. With parting words to Anne earlier, he'd promised her he'd be home by five o'clock. Promises meant nothing to her, she'd said. Pete thought differently, and now that a thread of trust was stretching between them, he didn't want to snap it.

He reached the elevator, wondering if the city's snowplows had cleared all the streets yet.

As the elevator doors opened, a grinning Tim faced him. A finger on the button, he held the doors open for Pete. "I didn't expect to see you until tonight at the birthday bash."

Pete joined him inside and leaned casually against a wall. "I had a few things to clean up."

"Who doesn't?" Tim grumbled about having to come in on Saturday to complete the details on a codicil for a will. "We're not the only ones putting in extra time here," he added. "Frank's burning the midnight oil like a recruit."

Pete wasn't surprised at that news. "He's hungry for the partnership."

"You aren't?"

Pete had no response that made sense. He'd thought he was, but lately he'd given little attention to it.

"Too busy with the family?"

"Well, we've been..." At Tim's smirk, Pete's voice trailed off. When had he begun to think of Anne and Rachel as his family?

A Cheshire cat grin lingered on Tim's face as he wandered out of the elevator. "See you tonight."

"Yeah." The elevator doors swooshed and closed. Everything between him and Anne was supposed to be temporary. She'd wanted it that way. He had, too. At least, he thought he had. But did he? he wondered.

Half an hour later, he entered the house. He called out to her, then heard the rushing water of the shower. With Anne's clothes scattered around, his neat bedroom looked like a cyclone had swept through.

Most of his childhood, he'd lived in similar chaos. Three boys sharing a room barely bigger than a closet had meant no one had a place for anything. He'd hated the lack of privacy, the disorder then.

Why were the years of what he'd done without finally dulling? Had he finally accepted that his father had never intended to hurt anyone? Only himself, Pete thought sadly, while he searched for his Levi's.

He found them on a chair beneath a peach-colored nightgown, a filmy silk he'd flung aside last night. From experience, he knew lust was fleeting. If only desire were all he felt, the answers would be simple. But more than passion had evolved between them. She brightened his day with her smiles, she warmed his night just by being near.

Changed into a sweatshirt and his jeans, he grabbed his jacket and headed for the door. Cold night air might clear his mind. He wandered outside, confused and uncertain. How was it possible to care so much for someone in such a short amount of time?

Anne ambled out of the shower to the scraping sound of the snow shovel. Outside, the sidewalks were carpeted with a fresh layer of snow. A knit cap pulled low over his ears, the collar of his pea coat shielding his neck, Pete was shoveling the driveway.

Like the man, his movements were aggressive and persistent. She'd seen flashes of impatience in his eyes, but he never lost an edge of control. That was her downfall with him. Calmly, relentlessly, he'd cut through her defenses and had stirred reminders that a partner, especially one in marriage, offered strength, a soul mate to rejoice with during life's good moments and to battle alongside of through the difficult ones.

Sighing, she settled before the mirror to apply makeup. Her own eyes held the truth. There was a glow to her face. She'd seen friends with the same look—when they'd fallen in love.

"Damn, it's cold."

Anne looked away from her own reflection to see Pete closing the front door.

"I called Norma and made sure she could watch Rachel tonight," he said, yanking off his cap and peeling out of his jacket.

A touch unsteady, she closed her compact. "Hope that I don't dump something in my lap this evening."

Pete rubbed hands still tingling from the cold. "Why would you?"

"Nerves do funny things to people."

Her anxiousness came through clearly to him. "You don't have to be nervous." In passing, his cold fingers grazed her neck.

Her mind filling with possibilities, she paused in reaching for her earring. What if she did something wrong and jeopardized what he'd been working for? "This is an important dinner to you, isn't it?"

"No more important than any other. But it is mandatory."

"And your friends will be there?"

"You've met them all," he reminded her while hanging his jacket on a hanger.

"They won't be any less surprised to see me."

Settling back against a dresser, he frowned. "What aren't you saying?"

"I'm sure they didn't expect to see me again."

"Then they will be surprised."

Anne crossed to the closet. A warning might be needed. Vividly she could recall one telling and dastardly moment right after her engagement to Keith. "When I first went to Keith's home, I committed faux pas all night. At one point, I was bored because Keith's father insisted on talking business. Even at a party, he couldn't forget business."

Mentally Pete grimaced. During the past seven years, he couldn't recall attending a party where business wasn't discussed.

"Well, anyway, I was bored and wanted to dance so I asked this rather stiff-backed, austere-looking man to dance. You know, someone who was older and hardly threatening in looks so Keith wouldn't get jealous."

The laughter in her voice alerted him. "Considerate of you."

"I certainly thought so." She slipped the dress over her head. "But Keith's sister Christina was shocked. She said I was so plebeian that I didn't even know lack of class when I stared at it," she mumbled from under the fabric.

Pete decided that he had little use for the snobbish Christina. "Could tell she was one of this world's sweeter people," he said when her head popped through the neckline of the dress. As she lifted her hair and offered her back to him, he took his cue. Lightly he skimmed his fingers over her bare back before reaching for the zipper. "Who did you ask to dance?"

"The butler."

With a chuckle, he bent his head and kissed her bare shoulder.

"It wasn't funny then." Despite her words, her eyes danced with a smile.

If he hadn't been hooked on this woman before, she would have lured him in that instant. God, but she was incredibly beautiful when happy. "I'm not worried. Don't you be."

Didn't he know worry came with motherhood? Anne wondered. She was becoming an expert at it. She managed a smile before he left the room because she knew he wanted to see it, but alone, she couldn't banish troubled thoughts.

In her swing, Rachel rattled colored discs. Lovingly Anne ran a light hand over her daughter's head. Not seconds ago, Pete had done the same thing.

"I could bring him trouble," she said softly to herself. Surely he realized that.

That evening as they stepped into the massive living room of Klein's Tudor-style home, Anne plastered a smile on her face, but nerves hadn't abated. Speculative stares coupling her and Pete roused a more intense uneasiness as she began to feel a rightness in being with him.

The mixture of soft and hard, strength and gentleness that were a part of him had captivated her from the beginning. And as he thrilled her, he scared her. Each day it was getting more difficult to imagine not being around him.

"You look beautiful." Reassuringly he placed a hand at the back of her neck and caressed it. *Beautiful* seemed a mild description in his mind. She looked downright sexy in a simple black dress that came high in front but dipped to a low V in the back.

How could he tell her that more than attraction bound him to her? Sure, he appreciated her beauty, sometimes sophisticated, sometimes youthfully innocent. She was a woman of great contrasts. Cool and aloof or warm and happy. Impulsive and cautious. Vulnerable and strong. Beneath smiles, he saw the fragile softness of a rose petal. Behind troubled eyes, he saw the determination and stamina of a dandelion. And always his head reeled just from looking at her.

Together, they inched their way around couples to reach the guest of honor. Silver gleamed and china shone on the long buffet table. Poised nearby, Amos Klein held court. Briefly they joined the well-wishers clustered around him then wandered to the buffet table.

A glass of champagne in her hand, Anne surveyed the tiny canapés, hot chafing dishes and a lobster mousse. Ahead of her, a woman with a linebacker's appetite for the miniature stuffed mushrooms and lobster quiches loaded her plate.

Pete cleared his throat impatiently.

The woman didn't notice.

"Forget the food." Tim sidled close beside him. "Did you hear what's happening?"

"I'm sure you're going to tell us," Pete mumbled back.

"Cassie is talking divorce. Seems she caught Marty and Janet together. I don't know the details."

Anne scanned the sea of faces until she found Cassie. A plastic smile didn't hide the woman's misery.

Anne's empathy for the sadness that would ripple over more than two people overrode her usual cynicism about marriage. "They have children, don't they?"

"A little girl," Tim told her, reaching around Pete to snitch a swipe at a pate. "Marty said he had to beg her to come with him tonight." Tim shook his head. "If she goes through with the divorce, the you-know-what will hit the fan."

"It's sad," Anne murmured, frowning.

Tim nodded. "I agree. But more than that, no one can ignore what a divorce will do to Marty's chances for the partnership."

Anne soon recognized that Tim's statement wasn't an unusual one. Throughout the evening, ambition floated on every sentence around her.

Munching on a scalloped melon slice, she passed pleasantries with the woman standing beside her. A large woman with highly bleached hair and a chubby face, she wore a bright orange-and-pink caftan that emphasized her extremely pregnant state. The woman's every other sentence pertained to her husband, Frank's career.

Bored almost to the point of yawning, Anne decided to take command of the direction of their conversation. "Do you have other children?"

"Two. We have two children." Pridefully she patted the swell in her dress. "And one more soon. A word of advice. For Pete's career, think about children soon."

Anne opened her mouth to protest the woman's misconception, then thinking of a better way, she laughed low. "Oh, I already have a daughter."

"You do?" She sounded absolutely jubilant as she asked, "You're divorced?"

"A widow."

As quickly as her smile formed, it gave way to a concerned frown, and her eyes darted to her husband.

For the past few minutes, he'd been leaning forward and looking past his wife and Anne to deliver subtle verbal jabs at Pete. With Anne's announcement, his words came out caustically, "Nothing like having a ready-made family, Pete. Klein will like that, as you know."

Anne shot a single stunned look at Pete.

He saw no point in clarifying their misconception. His private life wasn't anyone else's business. Clearly Anne thought differently. Pete noted her quietness, her forced smiles the rest of the evening. Uneasy, he could hear her unspoken questions. Before the evening ended, he knew that she'd insist on answers to the questions bothering her.

Anxious about the damn wall she was building between them, he took his time negotiating the car into the garage and walking Norma to her door.

Minutes later, when he entered the bedroom, Anne reacted predictably. "People have the wrong idea about us."

Pete settled on the edge of the mattress. Uncharacteristically, he tugged off a shoe instead of untying the laces. "Are you talking about Frank's not-too-subtle dig about a ready-made family?"

Standing in the middle of the room, she contorted to unzip her dress. "Yes." She frowned. "Obviously that's what I'm talking about."

He dropped one shoe then the other to the floor. He wanted to tell her that what other people thought about them didn't matter. But no fool, he knew that wasn't what she'd meant. She was challenging him for not clarifying their relationship. He didn't want to offer assurances to Frank or anyone that what he and Anne shared wasn't permanent. Hell, he didn't even want to think about that himself, he realized. At the rustle of silk, he looked up from unbuttoning his shirt. "Don't pay so much attention to him. Frank's worried."

Her dress floated to the floor. "About me?"

"About me." Standing, he yanked his shirt from his pants. "He believes marriage will tuck the partnership in my back pocket. If he wasn't already married, he would be in order to become partner," he said, trying to make her understand.

"You should have assured him that you're not—"

"Feeling anything for you?" He thought it incredible she'd say that when she stood before him in a wispy teddy that clung to every curve. "I couldn't do that."

The light in her eyes dulled. Too quiet, Pete mused. She was too damn quiet. There was so much he wanted to say, but how could he explain what he didn't understand?

Needing time alone, time to sort through her own feelings, Anne snapped up her robe. "I'm going to check on Rachel."

After doing so, she wandered through the kitchen to the back porch. Hugging herself, she stepped outside beneath the overhang. Puffs of snow hung precariously on the tips of evergreens. Light and unhurried, snowflakes filtered down around her. The quietness cocooned her, offered a serenity that conflicted with the turmoil inside her.

With his words, a pleasurable warmth had snuck up on her. Why did he have to make her feel so wanted? Why did she want to take his words to heart? She'd asked for no promises. So why was she almost yearning for them?

She never heard his approach, but a gentle hand, possessive and steady, snaked around her waist and drew her back against him.

"All night I've wanted to hold you like this," he whispered, splaying a palm over her belly.

So many times Anne had seen the heartbreak her mother had gone through because she believed in love. "Why couldn't you tell him?" she made herself ask.

The moment was wrong, too filled with tension to carry the discussion too far, to explore his own feelings too deeply. He toyed with the tips of hair brushing her shoulders. "He's much too sensible to understand that I've been swept off my feet by a beautiful woman."

Anne relaxed and rested her head back on his shoulder to watch a crescent moon spilling light through the edge of a passing cloud. "Swept off your feet?"

"That's what you've done," he murmured against the curve of her neck.

His voice was softer, huskier than usual, caressing her. She closed her eyes, shivered and pressed closer to him. Wrapped in his embrace, she was grateful for simple words lightly said. More serious ones would only force her to think. "It's cold out here. Should we go in?"

His hand shifted to the sharp angle of her hip. "Is Rachel okay?"

"She didn't stir—" Turning, she placed her hands not against fabric but his bare chest. Anne gathered the cloth of his opened shirt. "You're going to freeze out here."

"Warm me," he whispered.

His breath blended with hers on the cold night air, and eyes darker with passion locked with hers. As one kind of tension gave way to another, she floated her fingers upward to the strong column of his neck. "Do you think I'm the kind of woman who'll just fall into bed with you?"

His gaze followed the creamy flesh that narrowed at her throat and disappeared under the cloth of her robe. With a light kiss, he targeted a snowflake sparkling on the tip of her nose. "God, I hope so."

Three days passed. Schedules fell into place, as did a comfort between them. Anne had almost begun to forget that she wasn't in her own home, that Jerome wasn't still a threat. A nagging subconscience reminded her with a restless night. She awakened from a nightmare of one man standing with arms outstretched, grabbing for Rachel.

Before five she was awake again. Restless, she lay close to Pete for hours. Sleep must have come. When she opened her eyes, she blinked twice, not believing how late it was and scampered into motion.

The clock on the bedside table ticked away unmercifully fast. She swore at her own disorganization and laziness. Why hadn't she gotten up with the first ring of the alarm?

Half-dressed, she sat on the bed. To the sound of Pete bellowing out an off-key rendition of "When A Man Loves a Woman" over the sound of running water, she smoothed on panty hose, then slid on her skirt. Leaving the blouse hanging out, she dropped to her knees to search under the bed for her shoes.

A towel wrapped around his middle, Pete smiled at the view as he stepped from the bathroom. He dabbed a hand towel at the shaving cream on his jaw. "What are you doing?"

"I can't find my shoes." Her words came out muffled while she stretched farther under the bed. "Nothing is going right this morning. I think Rachel has a cold. She's really crabby."

Pete plopped onto the bed and lightly ran a hand over her raised bottom.

"I don't have time for that. If I don't—" Sitting back on her heels, she stared at the shoes hooked on his fingers. "You found them?" She pushed to a stand and joined him on the bed.

"You're not late yet." When she leaned forward to slip on her pumps, with a fingertip, he pushed back the hair draping her face.

She recognized mischief when she heard it. "I still don't have time for—you know."

Pete laughed. "Why are you so jittery?"

"I told you." Concern shadowed the brightness in her eyes. "I think Rachel has a cold and—"

He tossed the hand towel aside. "Level with me."

She took a few deep relaxing breaths. "It's only a matter of time before Jerome shows up." Unconsciously she gripped her hands together so tightly her knuckles whitened. "I have to call Christina."

So it wasn't them or him upsetting her. "And you dread it?"

"Yes. Even during good moments when I was married to Keith, she wasn't easy to talk to."

"Call her."

She stood and tucked in her blouse. "I will, but—"

"Now." Pete stood beside her and closed a hand tightly around hers. "What's the point in waiting?"

"A cowardly streak wants me to." She mustered up a weak smile but pressed her body against him, seeking some kind of support.

"Not you," he teased. Lazily he kissed her jaw. "Do it."

"That's not as easy as it sounds."

"But you'll do it."

She reared back and saw worry in his eyes. "Yes," she said with a long-suffering sigh.

He wasn't fooled. He'd begun to understand her. She weathered difficult moments by not taking them too seriously.

Though more nervous than she wanted to admit, Anne smiled mischievously as she skimmed a finger down his belly glistening with beads of moisture. She couldn't resist. With a quick turn away, she yanked the towel wrapped around his middle.

Naked, he lunged for her, but Anne dodged his hand, and with a low laugh, she rushed from the room toward the kitchen. Not giving herself time to ponder, she took a deep breath and punched out Christina's telephone number.

Disbelievingly, Anne listened to the maid. She was pleasant enough, but her message was blunt.

"Ms. Barrett is unable to receive your telephone call at present."

"When can she?" Anne insisted.

"I couldn't say, ma'am."

Until that moment, Anne hadn't considered the possibility that Christina would refuse. She slammed down the receiver and relied on herculean strength to stifle an urge to rush over to Christina's penthouse apartment and barge in.

"What happened?" Pete asked from the doorway.

"She won't even see me."

"Try again," he insisted.

Pete wasn't sure he'd given her good advice. From his brief encounter with Christina Barrett, he discerned she wouldn't make the moment easy or pleasant for Anne.

Slowly he strolled back to his office, a disposable coffee cup in his hand. He thought about a trademark infringement he should be working on, but his secretary had called in sick. Without her to type in changes on the document, there was no rush.

Eyes downward on the cup, he opened his office door then stared straight into Jerome Barrett's eyes.

"Mr. Hogan."

A rush of anger coursed through Pete. He smothered it. Venting it on Anne's behalf would be less beneficial than learning why Jerome had come.

"It's a small world," he said smugly.

Pete maintained a dispassionate look. "How did you know who I was?"

"My ex-daughter-in-law underestimates me, too." He scanned the framed degrees on the nearby wall. "My daughter seems to be acquainted with an old friend of yours. Geneva VanHern?"

Pete hadn't forgotten the meeting with Geneva and her friends. He'd thought it only a matter of time before Jerome showed up at his doorstep. Mentally Pete prepared himself for whatever plan Jerome had in mind.

"Learning your identity was easy."

Pete stopped at the front of his desk, set down his cup then perched on the edge of it. "Why am I important to you?"

"You may or may not be. I assume you're hiding her. My man knows none of her other acquaintances have her." He remained outwardly calm, but anger gripped his voice. "I came to give you a warning. I understand you're being considered for a partnership here." He paused, waiting, letting his words sink in before continuing. "As you know, Amos Klein is an old friend of mine."

Pete guessed Jerome's plan.

"A good or bad word to him could make the difference for you. If you don't stop hiding her, I'll make sure you never get the partnership."

Better men than you have tried to intimidate me, Pete reflected. He quelled his temper and an urge to answer the man with a hard right hook.

Jerome's smug grin widened. "I'd consider long and hard what I've said, if I were you."

Hell, yes, he did just that. And grew angrier.

Before Anne came home from work, he managed to resolve most of his fury via the rowing machine. Because he was tempted to pressure Anne into action, he kept quiet through dinner. But an hour of reasoning with himself changed his mind. Their best bet was Christina. And as long as Jerome's threat hung over their heads, nothing in her life, not even what existed between them, would be settled. "When are you going to see her?" he finally asked.

Anne closed the magazine she'd been fanning and pivoted away from the kitchen counter, offering him his mail. "I was going to see her tonight." She set his mail before him. "You know, even if I do talk to Christina, she may refuse to help."

Pete had planned to pace himself according to her mood, but dodging things had never worked for him. Stark reality had accompanied his childhood, had made him face obstacles head-on, always. "Why can't you go see her tonight?" he asked, riffling through the bills and junk mail.

Anne noted that he'd set aside, unopened, what looked like a wedding invitation. "Norma isn't home," she answered. "She has her tap dancing on Wednesday evenings."

"You go. I'll watch Rachel."

"You'll..." She arched a brow as if she found the idea questionable. "Pete, you don't know how to diaper her."

"Sure I do. I've watched," he returned, feeling male pride being punched at.

"Are you sure?"

"I know what has be done," he said defensively. But she wasn't even out the door yet when he regretted his offer. He didn't know anything about caring for a baby. Still, his bravado won out. "I throw a few drops of the milk on my wrist to test the temperature before I give her the bottle. The rest is a breeze."

Despite his cocky answer, Anne was still hesitant.

With his thumb, he ripped open the flap of an envelope and slipped out the invitation to his brother's wedding.

Anne peered over his arm. A pale peach rose and wedding rings were embossed on the invitation below words that carried a promise of forever. *For as long as I live, I'll love only you.* "It's beautiful." She waited for him to flip open the invitation. "Elizabeth Enterton and James Hogan." She wished them well. Some people found the happiness they were seeking. She hoped they did. "You only have a few days to get the RSVP back on time."

Pete tossed the invitation onto the rest of the mail. "I don't know if I'm going."

She thought she misunderstood him. "To your own brother's wedding?"

"We're not that close."

How could he say that? she wondered. Hadn't he been more father than brother to them? How could he spend all those years caring for his brothers and claim they weren't close? And if they weren't, why weren't they? Thinking of all he did for others, Anne decided it was time someone did something for him. "Why aren't you close to them?"

He frowned at her insistence. "They're busy. I'm busy," he said simply.

"You're too busy for the only family you have?" She couldn't hide her incredulity. For years, she'd longed for the very thing he was shunning.

"Why are you making a big deal out of this? They don't need me there."

Anne refused to relent. "Maybe they do."

The eyes that snapped at her were filled with annoyance. "This is none of your business."

"Ohh."

Instantly he knew he'd said the wrong thing.

She fired a penetrating look at him. "I see. You can tell me what to do, but if I question you about your life, well, then—"

He pushed back the chair and strode to the coffee-pot. "You don't understand any of this."

Anne frowned with annoyance. "I understand that you won't see your brothers. Why won't you?"

A coldness she'd never seen before iced his eyes. "Do you think they can forget all those years?"

Anne stared at him in disbelief, not believing he was blaming himself. "You weren't responsible for what they went through. They might have gone through more if it hadn't been for you."

"They don't need anything from me anymore." Pete steeled emotions he'd thought he'd left in his past. "Let's drop this."

Despite what he'd told her about his unsettled past, though he stood before her looking rock-solid, she'd heard the control in his voice slipping. Anne persisted. "You're wrong."

With an exasperated sigh, he faced her squarely, glints of annoyance still darkening his eyes. "Okay." His voice sounded flat. "What do you think they need from me now?"

Anne waited until his eyes met hers. "Friendship," she returned.

In the bedroom, Anne released the breath she'd been holding. She'd gone a step too far. She'd revived too much pain and bitterness. That wasn't her intention. She'd wanted to ease some of it, certain that he needed his brothers as badly as they needed them. Well, she'd handled the whole moment terribly, she decided. Nothing she said now would help. All she could do was let him mull over her words for a while. In the meantime, she had to deal with her own difficulty.

She returned to the kitchen with her coat. His back to her, he stood rigid, tense. Face your dragon, she mused. And I'll face mine. "If I'm not back by midnight, send out the reinforcements."

Pete whipped around to face her. "If you're not back in a few hours, I'll be on Christina Barrett's doorstep."

How she wanted to avoid the unpleasantness ahead and step into his arms. It was a temptation she resisted. "I'll hold you to that," she said with a strained airiness.

Pete stared after her. She hadn't understood about his brothers. He'd wanted to give them everything, he'd wanted to protect them from the hurt, and he'd given them nothing. But he was amazed at how much he could learn from her. Before she'd left, an uncertain smile had curved her lips, and there had been nothing hesitant in her voice or stance. In his whole life, he'd never met anyone with such grit.

Askance, he looked at Rachel. He was about to test his own. Babies didn't scare him, he thought firmly, as he recalled a comment Anne had once made.

Frowning, he swiped up a rattle from the floor and placed it on the cushion beside Rachel. Serene, her eyes closed, her head tilted to one side, she slept peacefully.

He splayed his hand. It was as large as her head. How could someone so diminutive, so sweet-looking worry him so much? For a moment, his confidence returned. He could handle a few hours of caring for her.

In seconds he learned what a fool he was. As if an alarm had gone off in her, Rachel's eyes opened wide and wandered around the room quickly. Without a

second of warning, her face changed from a soft milky
color to beet red. Her wail exploded in the air, her tiny
tongue wiggling as if it had been tickled, as she realized her mother wasn't near.

Chapter Eleven

Worried, Pete ran to her. Could she hurt herself if she turned redder? With effort, he stretched for a calm tone. "Ah, Rachel, come on," he cajoled. "This is new for me, too."

Amazingly she quieted, her attention riveting on him. Blessed silence lasted less than a second. Her bellow resumed, louder.

"Be patient," Pete soothed, as much to quiet her as to fight a wave of panic within him. Then he spotted the mop. He snatched it from the corner of the kitchen and stood it in front of him. To a captive audience, he played peek-a-boo through the strands.

Eyes wide, Rachel droned down to a whimper.

Sighing heavily, Pete slouched on a chair. Crisis

number one was over, but he wasn't so foolish as to believe there wouldn't be a second one.

It came an hour later.

Heating a bottle posed no problem. Any person with half a brain could boil water and warm a bottle, but how to hold a baby hadn't been taught at college.

He studied and analyzed the situation, then settled on the most logical method. Squatting over her, he held the bottle. Her little hands quickly curled around it as though she were starving.

Pleased with himself, he relaxed while she sucked away. Smugness definitely was man's downfall. Within minutes, the bottle squeaked empty, signaling another dilemma—picking her up. Anne usually patted her until she heard Rachel's soft burp, and odds were against him that she'd stay dry until Anne returned.

He gave himself a pep talk. He was an intelligent, well-educated, thirty-five-year-old man. He could pick up a baby.

Hovering close, he slid a hand awkwardly under her fanny and another beneath her shoulders, then slowly inched her up to his chest.

Head rearing back, she cooed, her eyes wide and studying him.

Pete chanced a smile. "Listen, kiddo, you're not the only one who's surprised here. Now, no squirming, because you are *definitely* dealing with a neophyte."

Cradling her, he untwisted the lid of the baby food jar. All seemed to be going well until he offered a spoon of the beets to her. Her nose wrinkling, she bubbled out the red mash. "Not fair, Rachel. Come on. This is what she left for you."

Sparkling brown eyes smiled back at him.

"Let's try again."

As he offered another spoonful, she rolled the food out off her tongue.

Pete was no masochist. He was already dotted with tiny red specks. "We're going to find something else. Let Mom feed you this one."

Anne's stomach flip-flopped while she waited in the foyer of Christina's apartment. When a door clicked open, the music of Mozart drifted to her. Anne ended her counting and swiveled around. She doubted Christina would be interested in knowing that there were one hundred and seventy-five small pink flowers on the wallpapered strip near the door.

"I didn't expect you to be so pesty."

Anne straightened her back. "I needed to talk to you."

She glided toward Anne, her chin lifted to an angle that was insulting. "We have nothing to discuss."

How many times had Anne pondered the woman's animosity? In the end, she had written it off as a dislike nurtured simply because of the difference in their family lineage. "Do you know what your father is doing?"

"I know he wants custody of Rachel. You should give it to him. He could offer her the kind of life you'd never manage. As Keith's daughter, she deserves it."

Anne stopped herself from fidgeting with her purse strap. "You don't understand."

She sent Anne a bored look. "I assure you I understand."

"No, you don't." Anger stormed Anne. "He's threatening to kidnap her."

Her quick, brittle laugh filled the air. "This is outrageous. You're becoming ridiculous, Anne." Her tone lowered, her face no longer etched with the feigned smile. "Our lawyer might be interested in your slander." She brushed past Anne and flung open the door.

Anne planted her feet.

"I don't know why I believed better of you." Fury brightened Christina's face. "You never belonged in our family. I thought my brother was insane to marry you. You were never good enough to be a Barrett. And now you're lying to cause our family more trouble."

Anne ignored her hateful censure. "I'm not lying. And even if you refuse to believe I'm telling the truth about your father, you do know the truth about Keith. Christina, you must tell your father. Tell him that I wasn't having an affair with Michael. Tell him about Keith's drinking. Your father is—"

"My father doesn't need to be hurt more," she snapped. "Do you think I'd tell him about Keith to save you?"

"Your father blames me for Keith's death."

"Perhaps you deserve blame," she said emotionlessly.

For all her bravado, Anne felt a tremble move through her. "This anger is hurting your father. If he knew the truth, he could heal. But he won't believe me. Christina, for his sake, tell him," she appealed before crossing to the door. "He's so grief-stricken that—"

"Don't tell me what he is. I know how hard he's taking Keith's death." As Anne passed her, she flared, "I don't want to ever hear more of your lies about my father."

With a resounding bang, the door slammed behind Anne.

Pete grimaced at the angry red rash on Rachel's backside. "Oh, man. Rachel. Bet that hurts like hell."

She giggled, snatching one foot in her hand.

"Well, it hurts me to look at it." He scanned the half dozen bottles and tubes on the bedside table. Placing a gentle hand on Rachel's chest to hold her in place, he shifted closer to read the bottles. Everything claimed a cure for diaper rash. Pete guessed that was the malady of the moment. "Okay, we'll try this one."

Rachel's foot found its way to her mouth.

"Hungry, huh?" He smeared gooey white cream on her bottom. If it wasn't the right stuff, he figured he couldn't do too much harm with one diapering. Awkwardly he brought the diaper into place. "I'll do the best I can to get this thing on right."

She smiled and gurgled as if giving him a vote of confidence.

More thumbs than fingers, he urged tiny arms and feet into what he guessed were pajamas. He fastened the last snap then gave himself a two-second lecture about courage before he gathered her again in his arms.

Contently she lay against his chest as he strolled toward the kitchen. There was no warning. Nothing to prepare him. Unexpectedly, suddenly, emotion swamped him. Dark eyes stared up at him, and his throat tightened. Memories flashed at him of years when he'd hugged his brothers through scraped knees and disappointing holidays. He'd stared into other eyes then that had sent him the same look. A look of unconditional trust—a look that had made him feel as if he were the only person in the world.

Pete stilled and lowered his head to kiss her forehead. A warmth he hadn't known in years was suddenly inside him again. Ironically he'd thought that he'd known what he wanted in life, but one little girl had just made him wonder if that was true.

Anne wrestled with anger during the drive from Christina's. Her irritation hadn't eased away by the time she opened the back door.

Passing through the kitchen, she noticed the full jar of beets and felt her annoyance shifting from Christina to Pete. Hadn't he fed Rachel? Anne scowled at the cellophane wrapper from a cream-filled sponge cake and rushed toward the bedroom. If he'd fed her a junk snack—

The thought hung unfinished.

At the bedroom doorway, she froze. Pete sat in a chair by the window and cradled a sleeping Rachel as if she were his own.

Anne's heart twisted. Tears welled up before she could block them. Swallowing hard against the knot in her throat, she damned her own weakness. But this wasn't fair. How did she remember to keep her heart guarded when her daughter was lovingly embraced in his arms?

"You're back," he said low, not to disturb Rachel.

Conversation promised the only way to arrest emotion. Anne strolled closer and slid off her coat. She had to resist. She couldn't allow a tender moment between a caring man and her daughter to touch her too deeply. "I noticed the jar of beets on the counter. Didn't you feed Rachel?"

Pete caught the flare of annoyance in her voice and excused it to a bad encounter with Christina. "I gave her pears. We decided that beets weren't in her best interest."

We. Anne felt her strength ebbing away again, her willpower vanishing. An ache, an unsatisfied need, passed through her. She chased it away immediately, but she couldn't overlook that something had happened while she was gone. Pete had found a part of himself that he'd left behind years ago. Anne had never doubted his capacity to love was deep and sensitive. She'd felt it in his touch and sensed it when he'd talked about his brothers. She'd seen it in him every time he helped others. Only he'd forgotten it existed.

"Hey?" Her daughter was still nestled against his chest. "What happened with Christina?"

With a shake of her head, she turned on the water spigot at the bathroom sink.

Pete had hoped for progress with Barrett's daughter. All day, he'd avoided adding to Anne's trouble, avoided telling her about the scene with Jerome in his office. Bent over the crib, he lowered Rachel to the mattress and waited for Anne to reappear in the bathroom doorway. "I guess it's a bad news day," he said with some lightness, hoping she'd take what he had to say the same way. "Jerome came to see me."

She nearly dropped the glass in her hand. "Here?"

"At the office."

"Why?" she yelled in an appeal to a greater power. Oh, she'd been foolish, she realized. Stupid. Or she'd have been prepared for Jerome's harassment to spill over into Pete's life. "I'm so tired of him disrupting my life. And now he's doing it to yours, too. What did he want?"

She looked pale, the light in her dark eyes shadowed. "Nothing important," he lied impulsively. "He was looking for any ally."

Anne couldn't keep the alarm out of her voice. "He knows I'm here then."

Pete inched closer. Wasn't this why he'd skirted telling her? He'd known she'd feel trapped again, believe his home no longer offered sanctuary. "He knows we're together. That's all he knows."

"Isn't that enough?" Walls seemed to be closing in on her, and Anne didn't know how to stop them. "He'll come here."

Sitting, he patted the mattress. "Why don't *you* come here?"

Weak legs carried her to him. When he grabbed her hand and tugged her down beside him, she couldn't resist. A mental weariness was draining her. She was tired of the trouble, of always looking over her shoulder.

"You asked for no promises. This time I'm making one." When she didn't face him, he cupped her shoulders and twisted her toward him. "He isn't going to get her."

Anne wanted to believe him. Lord, she wanted to. She wanted to feel protected, to lean on someone just a little. He pressed his forehead to hers as if to share her troubled thoughts.

"Believe me," he insisted. There was more truth in his words than she'd imagine. Since she and her daughter had entered his life, he had changed. His needs and wants weren't the same anymore. For days, one emotion had badgered him. The time was past pretending that she could walk out the door tomorrow and everything would be the same as before for him. "Do you believe me?" he asked against her temple.

A desperation she'd never known made her cling to him. "Yes, I believe you," she whispered. She pressed her lips to the mouth close to hers and tightened her arms around him. The kiss was quick in comparison to others, hardly a kiss, a brush of his lips, but he made the storm rage through her again. And the mouth on hers made her forget. More than anything she wanted that at the moment.

Lying back, she drew him with her, seeking to absorb his strength and determination. She slithered her fingers beneath his shirt and tugged it from his pants. As she traced a path down the rock hardness of his stomach and eased down the zipper at his pants, she heard his soft groan. Need, not want, led her. She needed him. She knew the danger in needing anyone too much, but at the moment, she didn't care.

With wild abandonment, she urged him, arching her hips and pressing against him, grinding into him. She didn't want gentleness. She yearned for the slick texture of his damp skin on her, needed roughness to overpower the numbness threatening to take hold.

One item at a time, he tossed aside her clothes, pausing only to skim exposed flesh. A humming began in her head as his mouth sought her breast. Moist and warm, his tongue enticed more than her skin. Almost desperately, she longed for the mindless haze to sweep over her. She closed her eyes and gave in to the pleasure and torment as a downpour of emotion rushed through her veins. With a flutter of his fingers, the brush of his lips, a flick of his tongue, she sank deeper beneath a spell only he seemed capable of casting over her. Whatever he wanted, she thought. She wanted whatever he wanted.

Pete let her moans guide him. He'd meant only to comfort, but there was a sudden urgency in her, a fire.

His mind filling with her scent, her taste, her touch, he couldn't slow down the storm sweeping over him. Hands that meant to be gentle bruised with urgency. A servant to his own needs, he gasped her name in reverence and drew her to him, not wanting to ever let her go as the frenzy enveloped him.

Wild, they strained against each other, her softness blending into him. Whatever separated them during the daylight hours disappeared now beneath the glow of the moonlight. With a generosity that stunned him, she opened more than her body to him. A promise even she might not be aware of whispered on the air. All the denials he'd ever heard from her were silenced as flesh melded. And he wanted all he could have with her. All the pleasure, all the sensations, all the loving that was possible.

The frenzy of the night lingered even as shafts of morning sunlight lightened the room. Anne reclosed her eyes and lay still, hovering at the edge of wakefulness. The scent of love clung to her, wrapping her in a cocoon. She felt safer with him, more secure than she had in her whole life. No one had ever given her that gift. With his firmness, his strength, he made her believe everything would be all right.

"Come on, sleepyhead," Pete cajoled, smoothing a hand over her backside. "It's time to wake up. Got a surprise for you."

Reluctantly, lazily, Anne shoved the pillow aside and forced herself to roll over.

Grinning, he stood alongside the bed with a breakfast tray in his hand, then eased down to sit beside her. "Don't look so scared."

Anne grazed his cheek with a knuckle. Too well she knew what his cooking ability was like. Dubiously she aimed a look at the breakfast tray. How could she refuse his breakfast without hurting his feelings? Fully awake now, she said as an excuse, "I don't have time for breakfast in bed. I have to get up and feed Rachel."

"I already did."

Anne mentally groaned, dreading what was under the napkin on the tray. She tucked back strands of her hair and mustered a smile, preparing herself.

"Voilà!" He whipped the napkin away from the plate.

The sight of fluffy scrambled eggs, a dish of fresh fruit and a golden brown croissant did more than amaze her. It rumbled her stomach in anticipation. More eager, Anne fluffed a pillow behind her then popped a strawberry into her mouth. "Mmmm. Are you trying to spoil me?"

"That's the idea. Now, start eating and I'll be right back."

While he was out of the room, Anne dove the fork into the eggs enthusiastically. During her childhood, she'd never been pampered. Independence was expected, was a necessity. Everyone was too busy—always. The only time she'd had breakfast in bed was in the hospital after she'd had Rachel.

"Coffee is coming," he called out.

A forkful hung in midair with his announcement. Suddenly she couldn't help but laugh. She knew this was too good to be true. His coffee was dreadful.

"Here it is." Eyes downward on the tray in his hands, Pete strode slowly toward the bed with a carafe and two cups.

Anne feigned an idiotic grin. "Oh, good, coffee." She dared to ask. "Did you really make this breakfast?"

"Norma," he said, inching the cup closer.

A pleasant rich aroma floated to her. "Thank goodness." Her eyes skimming his tie, she offered him a strawberry. "You're dressed."

His frown mirrored hers. "Were you hoping I wouldn't be?"

With a fingertip, she stroked a corner of his mouth. "Guess I'll have to wait until—"

"Four o'clock." He bent forward and kissed her. She tasted like strawberries.

"Not soon enough."

"No, it isn't," he murmured, tempted to say to hell with everything but her.

Anne released a low, husky laugh against his lips. "Now I understand. You had an ulterior motive for bringing me breakfast in bed?"

"Hopefully."

"Oh, all right." She feigned a grudging look. "I'll buy pizza tonight."

"I had something else in mind."

She nipped at his ear. "That comes later."

* * *

Just barely Pete hung on to his concentration through three morning meetings. Back in his office at two in the afternoon, he was facing a mountain of work when Frank strolled in.

"I'm supposed to discuss the Bentley merger with you." He dropped a contract in front of Pete.

Pete felt irritation rise. Was Frank so confident he had the partnership in the palm of his hand that he'd already begun barging in on any of his colleagues without calling first? As a patience he'd nurtured through the years threatened to slip away, he considered it luck when his intercom buzzed. He answered, taking the needed seconds to quell his temper.

Twice, Frank glanced at his watch while Pete listened to the caller. "I only have a few minutes," Frank said low and impatiently. "I have a new client coming."

Pete was already handing him the phone. "It's for you, Frank. Some emergency at home."

Frank glared at the receiver in the manner of someone ready to yank the cord from the wall. Again he glanced at his watch. "Well, it's not that serious, is it?" he questioned the caller. "Then you handle it." He sounded exasperated. "I can't leave. A new client is coming. You know which one."

So did Pete. Mr. Megabucks.

"My mother-in-law," he explained in an offhand tone to Pete. "Everyone is acting ridiculous. I've been to the hospital two times already with my wife for false labor. That's all this is, too."

"Maybe you should go. This could be the big moment."

"I have too much going on here to sit around a hospital waiting room and learn it's another false alarm." He shrugged a meaty shoulder. "When I get home, I'll have to listen to a lecture about my not having time for them. She's wrong, of course, not to comprehend that I can't let anything come before this. You understand. You're working harder, too."

No, he hadn't been.

"Work comes first," Frank insisted.

While Frank expounded about the possibility of a hostile takeover at Bentley's company, Pete gave him a long look. At one time, hadn't he been as single-minded about his career? But was it really worth sacrificing everything else for?

At four o'clock as he'd promised, Pete was already home. While he was exercising, Anne tossed clothes into the washing machine. Though she wouldn't have held him to his morning promise or any other, she realized she felt pleased that he'd kept it.

Flicking on the washer, she could hear the syncopated thumping sound of the rowing machine from the other room. Everything in her life was running smoothly for the moment despite her failed attempt to enlist Christina's help.

But how would she get Jerome to listen? Anne wondered, turning in response to the chime of the doorbell. She couldn't stay at Pete's forever. At some moment, what they were sharing would be over. When that moment came, she didn't want him to feel trapped because her life was still in limbo.

Anne made the exchange of money for the pizza carton and only briefly eyed the load of clothes that needed ironing.

In the bedroom, his legs bent, Pete rowed with a steady rhythm. Perspiration soaked his gray sweat-shirt and beaded his forehead while he kept an eye on the video that was playing. This evening he was rowing across the Rhine River.

Content, Rachel was watching the show, too— namely him.

Anne cleared her throat to get his attention. "Your muscles are bulging."

"They're supposed to."

"And is your face supposed to turn red, too?"

"Did you come in here to critique my technique?" he asked between breaths.

"No, I came to tell you that the pizza is here."

"Thank goodness. I'm about ready to fold."

"Why didn't you stop?"

"Couldn't," he managed, then grunted. "Made a promise to do this until the pizza arrived."

"Well, it's here. And if you don't come, I'm eating it all."

Anne returned to the kitchen and set out plates and napkins, but several minutes passed before she heard the shuffle of Pete's sneakers on the hallway floor. "What took so long?"

He had Rachel cradled against his chest. "She was indisposed."

"Lucky you."

"Have you noticed that she does that more when I'm alone with her?"

He looked so deadly serious that she couldn't help smiling. "You're imagining things."

"And it was green."

Wisely she stifled a laugh while setting the pizza on the table.

"Sweet little thing, aren't you?" He nuzzled Rachel, drawing her giggle. "But a little cranky today. Don't you think she's been cranky?"

"That's normal." Anne balanced a slice of pizza on her palm. "She was running a slight fever."

He didn't take that news lightly. "Fevers usually mean something is wrong." He sat across from her. "You should take her to the doctor."

Anne stared in amazement at him. He was usually so calm, a pillar of strength. "You're being a worry-wart."

"I'm being sensible," he countered. "If she's running a fever, then—"

"Relax," Anne mumbled between chews. "She's all right."

"How do you know she really is?" he asked, smoothing a hand over Rachel's head.

"I know she's fine." Anne tilted her head to look at her daughter's face. "Make that face that causes her to laugh."

Pete frowned. "Which one?"

"You know that disgusted expression you have when I'm not listening to you?"

"She laughs at that?"

Anne smiled. "So do I. Make it."

Pete gave it his best try.

On cue, Rachel giggled.

"See it," Anne said in a delighted tone and pointed at Rachel's mouth.

Amazement edged his voice. "It's a tooth, isn't it?"

"Uh-huh."

In wondering awe, he kept staring at Rachel's mouth, marveling at the chip of white protruding through her daughter's gum. "I'll be damned."

Anne leaned back on suddenly weak legs. Her heart hammered in her chest as she stared at him. Never had she expected to see a look of pride in any man's face when he stared at her daughter. A tight band across her chest threatened to snatch the breath from her if she didn't move away.

In a rush of movement, she hurried to the refrigerator and buried her head in it on a pretense of reaching for a soda. Unexpected tears smarted her eyes.

Disregard the moonlight and soft caresses. It was the everyday moments that had weakened her resolve. She'd tried to ignore her feelings for him and even his caring manner with Rachel, but how could she not be moved when he lovingly smiled at Rachel or held her tightly to his chest or beamed at the discovery of a tooth? Moments like this one carried so much of what she longed for and made her face what she'd tried to deny. She'd fallen in love. Despite all her efforts not to, she was in love with him.

"Well, Rachel, pretty soon I'll be able to introduce you to the wonderful world of fast foods. Hamburgers with onions, and greasy French fries and chocolate chip cookies."

His light, airy tone roused Rachel's giggle.

With the back of her hand, Anne brushed tears from her cheeks and straightened, turning to level a tough look at him. "And apples, and carrots and—"

Pete rolled his eyes. "Sometimes you sound just like a mother."

She managed to match his smile before she looked back in the refrigerator. She couldn't let emotion win, she reminded herself, pushing aside soda cans to find Rachel's formula. "Damn," she murmured as her search proved futile.

"Such language." He clucked his tongue. "Tender ears are listening."

"I'll remember to keep her away from you when you're shoveling snow." Sighing, Anne slammed the refrigerator door and looked out the window. Snowflakes rushed toward the ground. It was a good evening to stay home, but maybe she needed some time to herself even if it meant venturing out in traffic snarled by the weather. "Since you're such an old hand at baby-sitting, would you mind watching Rachel a few more minutes?"

"I don't mind, do I?" He smiled at Rachel. "We'll play pattycake—if I can remember the rhyme."

"How can a man be near genius and not know nursery rhymes?" she teased, trying not to think too much.

His huge hands enveloped her daughter's small ones. "I led a sheltered life."

"Well, try to remember, because you'll be on your own. I have to go to the store for formula."

"You stay." Grabbing another quick bite of pizza first, he shoved back his chair. "It's snowing again. I'll go."

Anne fought to bring a light sound to her voice. "Want to pick up a video?"

In passing, he caught her at the waist and pulled her back to nuzzle her neck. "Anything you want." He left the room for a second and came back into the kitchen with his parka half on. "Which one?"

"I've always been fond of *Three Men and a Baby*."

His eyes narrowing, he pinned her with a fake threatening look. "Don't I give you enough laughs?"

"Sometimes," she teased as a longing filled her to believe in something as fragile as love.

"Pick another."

Anne tilted her head up to him. *"Ghost."*

He kissed her quickly. "Again?"

"I like it." Love eternal seemed almost like fantasy to her, but she always enjoyed the movie, never failed not to cry at least twice.

"Make popcorn," he called from the doorway.

Chapter Twelve

Pete wandered down three aisles in the grocery store before he found the shelves packed with formula and diapers. Frowning, he perused the shelf before him for the brand name Anne used.

"Oh, I love it when new fathers do the shopping," a scratchy voice said behind him. The clerk, a small woman with a mass of gray curls, had smiled amiably at him when he'd entered the store. "A boy or girl?"

"A girl." Pete saw no point in telling her the child wasn't his. He knew another woman with the same kind of exuberance about babies and animals. Lolita gushed over them, catered to them, believed they made more sense than most adults.

He, for one, was grateful for that. Had Lolita not been around for him during some bleak moments in his life, he wouldn't be who he was today. She'd been his solace whenever his father had drunk too much. With his brothers' hands in his, Pete had raced often down the hallway to Lolita's apartment with a claim he wanted to see her cats. She'd known better, but she'd never said a word.

She'd ushered them into her apartment, and before they'd left, they'd been stuffed with homemade cookies, the same chocolate-chip cookies her sister Norma was still mothering him with.

"How old is she?" the clerk asked.

Pete, intent in his search, didn't answer the question. "This is the right one," he stated, as he reached for a can.

"Oh, good, you remembered what kind."

Nodding, he eyed the small, stuffed teddy bear on the shelf below the cans.

"One can or two?"

"Two. And this," he added, handing her the teddy bear.

Mechanically Anne took a bag of popcorn from the kitchen cupboard and crossed to the microwave. Now she'd really done it. Love? She gave her head a shake in disbelief. She'd sworn she wouldn't let that happen. She should have seen it coming. She'd begun to depend on him, to need him, to share too much with him.

She strolled toward the living room. Setting Rachel in her playpen, Anne heard the slam of a car door. She hadn't expected Pete back so soon. Had he forgotten the brand name for the formula? A tease riding her tongue, she looked out the living room window. Tension clutched at her stomach. Jerome stood beneath the streetlight, flurries rushing down around him.

Anne wheeled around to rush to Rachel and gather her in her arms, then stopped herself. She couldn't panic. She couldn't give into fear. For Rachel's sake, she had to take control of the situation. Anne racked her brain for a solution. Only one came to mind.

Christina's maid tried to brush her off again.

Anne wasn't about to take no for an answer. "Tell her to talk to me, or I'm calling the police and having her father arrested."

Only a few seconds passed before Christina greeted her with indignation. "Who do you think you are?"

"Save the Princess Christina act this time," Anne insisted. "Your father is at my door. I've had enough of this. I want you to come over here and tell him the truth. You know the truth, Christina. You're the only one he'd believe."

"We've had this discussion before. I haven't changed my mind. I don't intend to tell my father anything. In fact, if he wants to take you to court and fight for Keith's daughter—"

"*My* daughter," Anne flared.

As if anything Anne had to say was inconsequential, she went on, "If my father wants Rachel, I'll do everything in my power to help him."

"Fine," Anne said calmly. "You do whatever you want, but I plan to, too. If you don't come over here and explain everything to him *now,* I'm calling the police. That's not simply a threat."

Mirthlessly Christina laughed. "Do you expect the police to believe some fantasy about him trying to kidnap Rachel?"

"Oh, they probably won't," Anne agreed. "But that's not the only phone call I plan to make. After I call them, I'm calling the newspaper. I'm sure they'll be interested in any kind of news concerning Jerome Barrett. Maybe they'll even send a photographer and a reporter."

A deadly silence answered Anne.

What would she do if Christina didn't take her words seriously? Anne pressed harder. "You decide."

"Where are you?"

"Not far from you." Anne rambled Pete's address. "You have only fifteen minutes. If you're not here by then, I'm calling the newspapers."

A dial tone resounded in her ear, and Anne gripped the phone tighter. Through the window, she could see Jerome climbing the steps. She had two choices. If he was out there when Pete came home, she didn't know what would happen. It would be better to let him in. Talk to him. If they could carry on a civil conversation, she might be able to reason with him. Regardless, his daughter was on her way.

Tension and apprehension accompanying her, Anne flung open the door.

Jerome greeted her with a tight, unpleasant smile. "Did you think I wouldn't find out where you were?"

"Jerome, come in."

First puzzlement, then wariness flashed in his eyes.

"Please." Anne opened the door wider. Taking a deep breath, she prepared herself for the next few minutes. This man had already lost his son. Yet, she'd have to hurt him, or she'd lose Rachel. "Please, sit down. We need to talk."

"I have little to discuss with you." His disapproval of her sliced through the air. He started to turn away, then his eyes settled on Rachel. Unexpectedly they warmed with a brightness Anne hadn't seen in them since before Keith's death.

With stunning clarity, Anne recognized what she'd been too preoccupied to notice. He loved Rachel. All this time, she'd viewed his wanting Rachel as nothing more than a power play. Now she knew differently. Did he see that she had Keith's smile? Did he notice that her hair curled around her ear like Keith's had?

"She belongs with me," he said almost calmly. "I can offer her an upbringing suitable for a Barrett."

"Happiness can't always be found with money. It never brought much to Keith."

Anger rose in his voice again. "You mean you didn't!"

Anne touched the arm of the chair beside her as her legs threatened to buckle beneath her. "You gave him everything, but he wasn't happy. He never understood love," she appealed. "Jerome, I don't even know if he understood how to do anything but take."

His features hardened to a stony expression. "Who are you to tell me about my son?"

"I was his wife. I know what he couldn't give."

Snow turned to sleet as Pete made the final turn onto his driveway. Was it only a few weeks ago his life had been so different? His wanting Anne had never been questionable. From the first kiss, he'd accepted the desire simmering within him, but something else had happened to him.

His feelings had changed for her. He'd never denied the attraction, then the wanting and the need, but now he couldn't imagine a day without her.

Pete opened the car door and laughed at the night air. With the same velocity as the wind beating at his back, a revelation slammed at him. He loved her.

Dammit, he really loved her.

He'd gone most of his life not making promises to anyone and suddenly wanted them from one particular woman. What had made him believe that he was a solitary man, needing no one else? Childhood pain was the obvious answer. Loving anyone too much risked the heart. He'd watched his father fall apart because of love, so he'd rejected the idea of marriage. But he finally realized what he'd failed to see all those years. Love wasn't an emotion a person could flick off.

He closed the car door and locked it. Now what? he wondered. How did he deal with something he thought he never wanted in his life? He couldn't walk away from it and pretend it didn't exist just because he didn't want it to. More important, how did he tell

Anne that he wanted the one thing with her that she'd placed at the top of some "never" list—marriage?

Pete was still tossing thoughts around when the approaching headlights of a car glared in his eyes. The Saab pulled up to the curb behind a Mercedes already parked in front of his house.

His heart drumming, Pete watched as a tall woman slid out from behind the steering wheel. Though the collar of her coat was raised and shielding her face, he remembered the chestnut-colored hair of the woman in the restaurant who'd frozen Anne with a look.

He sprinted across the icy surface of packed-down snow, his feet slipping beneath him, and charged up the steps past Christina. From the house, he could hear a man's voice raising.

"I've listened to enough of this," Jerome yelled. "I'm taking my granddaughter."

Anne dashed toward the playpen to block his path to Rachel.

"No, you're not taking her," Pete countered from the doorway.

Standing sideways between the two men, Anne darted a look from one man to the other.

His face flushed with fury, Jerome met Pete's challenge with more anger. "She's my granddaughter."

Anne held her breath as they measured each other, and for a long moment neither man moved.

"Father," Christina insisted, stepping into the house. "We have to leave." She lunged forward and grabbed his arm. "She's made threats."

Balking, he didn't move an inch. "What kind of threats?"

"To call the newspapers."

He shrugged off his daughter's leather-gloved hand. "Let her. Let the world know what a tramp she is."

The bag dropped from Pete's hand. From the corner of her eye, Anne saw him moving quickly. The moment was too explosive for her to let her own pride get in the way. "Pete, it's all right," she said in a rush and stepped into his path.

"It's not all right," he flared.

Though Jerome cast him a wary glance, he baited. "So you've found a new lover quickly."

"Please," Christina begged. "We have to leave. If we don't, she'll tell everyone about Keith, about—" As her father swung a look back at her, her mouth hung open with an awareness that she'd said too much.

"What about Keith?" he demanded.

"He—he did drink a little."

"I know that. Do you think I'm stupid or blind?" Hostility again hardened his voice. "She wasn't a decent wife to him."

"That's—" Christina paused as if the words were caught in her throat. "That's not true."

Looking stunned, Jerome rounded to face her. "You told me that Keith came to see you and was furious because he knew about her affair. You told me—"

"I lied."

"You lied about what? The affair?"

"Everything."

He paled, disbelief giving way to a pain that seemed almost unbearable.

Anne looked away. No one deserved such agony. Regardless of all the trouble Jerome had caused her, he didn't deserve this.

"I'm sorry." Christina spoke softly as if frightened to jar him from private thoughts. "I've always protected him," she tried to explain. "I knew he was drinking and that he was seeing other women."

Jerome blanched. "*He* was the one, not her?" When she reached out for him, he shook her hand away. "Leave me be." His stare whirled on Anne, not his daughter. "You never lied?" Incredulity still clung to his voice.

"No," she answered softly. Anne wondered if she'd ever seen pain quite so visible before on a person's face. She found no satisfaction in this moment. She'd longed for him to learn and accept the truth about his son. Now she wished for some other way, any way that could have kept Keith's memory as it was in his father's mind.

Paler, he appeared a decade older than the proud, arrogant man who'd entered the house minutes ago. He lumbered toward the door, then stopped. Anne expected no apology. It wasn't his style. But his words echoed with one. "I know nothing I can say will change anything but...you will let me see her, won't you?"

Fear and wariness made her want to deny him anything, but she knew if she didn't take the first step now in trusting him, then Rachel would never know her grandfather. "Yes. You can see her." Anne gave him a thin smile. "Just call first."

The closing of the door signaled the finality of what had been a nightmare for her. Sadness, relief and exhaustion swept through her. "That poor man."

Pete locked his hand with hers. "He had to learn the truth someday."

"I know, but I feel as if I sliced a piece out of his heart."

He tipped her chin up. "You're not the one who did that."

No, Keith had, Anne acknowledged, but as a parent, she empathized with Jerome's sadness and disappointment and loss.

"Anne, you couldn't prevent any of this."

She shook her head at his softening tone. "I know." As he slipped an arm around her shoulders, she raised her chin. "I didn't make the popcorn yet," she said almost apologetically.

He nearly laughed, then realized this was a typical Anne move, a way to break free of troubled thoughts. "Well, I got the video. Now you can have a good cry."

Anne played along to lift her own spirits. "You could have pretended you didn't notice."

"Yeah, I could have," he bantered.

The weight from months of worry lifting from her, she didn't miss the distress shadowing his eyes. Playfully she punched him in the right arm. "Yeah." Anne grinned impishly, almost daringly and raised her fists. "Want to play?"

At her pugilistic pose, he broke into laughter and raised his hands in surrender. "I give."

"That's more like it." Her words came out with a squeal as he grabbed her and tumbled her back to the sofa with him. "Sort of," he murmured against her mouth. Holding her tight on top of him, he stared up at smiling dark eyes, eyes he wanted to spend the rest of his life looking at. He wanted to wake up beside her, listen to her off-key singing from the shower, go grocery shopping with her again. He needed her, not just her body. He needed her with him every minute of his life. "I love you," he said softly.

Light faded from her eyes almost instantly. As she tensed against him, as he felt her heart quicken, he started to tighten his hold on her.

She squirmed away and scrambled to stand. She didn't dare speak. Panic burned her throat. He wasn't supposed to say those words. Unbelievably she realized she'd never prepared herself for the future, for what would happen if she ever settled the problem with Jerome. "We agreed to no commitment, no strings, no promises." Pressure in her chest made breathing suddenly difficult. God, but she wanted it all with him and was afraid to grab for it. She backed away from him as if he carried some communicable disease. "Don't—"

"Don't what?" He rose quickly. Too tempted to grab her, he tucked his fingers into the short pocket of his Levi's. "Don't love you? That's impossible."

She stepped backward, wanting distance, needing it, aware that if he took her in his arms she'd crumble. "You're complicating everything."

Frustration and anger snowballed inside him even as he reminded himself that she was reacting predictably. From the beginning, she'd leveled with him. He'd accepted her words then, believing they echoed his feelings. But that was before. This was now. Now he wanted her. He needed her, and he believed she needed him. "Your life wasn't simple when you came here."

Anne circled to the other side of the coffee table. "I thought we understood each other."

Pete shifted a shoulder to resist the muscle bunching from the tension of the moment. "We did understand each other. I changed my mind," he said far more calmly than he felt. "I want to get married."

"Married?" Anne took another step back. She'd thought he might want to live together, but he wanted it all. Why would he? He'd always seemed to shun the idea of marriage. Why now? As painful as one thought was, Anne allowed it to form. For his career, marriage was a must. "You only think you want a wife now because of your job. The partnership—"

Patience snapped. He rounded the table in two strides and gripped her shoulders. "To hell with the partnership. Is that what you think this is about? I want to marry you because I love you."

Anne drew a shuddery breath. He loved her. He really loved her. She spun away, offering him her back, afraid to look at him, afraid he'd see the longing in her eyes. "I was lousy at marriage."

Pete couldn't think beyond the moment, but he knew what she'd said was a lie. "No. He was."

Without forewarning, tears threatened. Anne closed her eyes and swallowed hard against the knot in her throat.

"Do you love me?"

Though she felt him close behind her, she still jumped when his hands cupped her shoulders.

"Anne?"

She pressed her lips together. How could she lie? What stunned her was how it had happened in such a short amount of time. "What we feel for each other isn't enough."

"What else matters?" he asked angrily.

"You don't understand, do you?" Anne stretched for a quick, calming breath and swung around, side-stepping him. "You said no promises." How could she make him understand? "Marriage is for other people."

Pete frowned, baffled. She was an intelligent, strong-willed woman, a woman too capable of giving to shut off feelings. He searched for words to penetrate her resistance. "You've been here for weeks. We're living together now. If we married—"

"Rachel would get too attached to you."

"Is that so bad?" he asked, not comprehending why she found that so offensive.

All of a child's pain surfaced within her again. Those years of feeling unwanted, of longing for someone to care enough about her to stick around, closed in on her as if they were yesterday. "Yes, it is. I don't want her to go through what I did. None of the men my mother married wanted another man's child," she yelled. "I didn't realize that. I kept thinking I had a father."

An ache for her and himself skittered through him as he felt her slipping away from him. "They weren't all like that, were they?"

"No." Torment darkened her eyes. "But none of them were permanent. They were in my life for a little while, then gone forever. Once my mother divorced them, not one of them came around to see me again. Not one of them ever really cared about me." With effort, she swallowed hard. "I won't put Rachel through that. She's better off with no father, than believing she has one and being hurt, waking up one day and watching him walk out of her life forever and never looking back."

"I'm not going to walk away."

Anne battled a longing to believe him, to believe in them. "You told me there are no guarantees."

He raised his hands, palms out to her. "I can't give you one. But—"

She saw the hurt in his eyes, too much hurt. Furious with herself, she wheeled around toward the bedroom. A twinge of doubt touched her heart. She didn't give herself time to think about it and grabbed a suitcase.

Pete thought of following her, of yelling at her, of shaking her, of cajoling, of begging. Instead, he paced in front of the window. Nothing she said made sense to him. If they loved each other, what else was important? Didn't she know that he wouldn't make a promise that he didn't plan to keep? He wouldn't hurt her or Rachel. He wasn't any of those other men. He knew how much a child could be harmed when a father turned away.

Anne buttoned her coat then took several blankets for Rachel before reentering the living room.

"You're leaving now?" Anger edged his voice. "That's dumb."

Anne bundled Rachel, then grasped the suitcase again. "No, what was dumb was my coming back here. I should have known better. Rachel and I would only—"

"Just stop there." He slashed a hand through the air. "What it comes down to is—"

"Is Rachel." Anne faced him, resolving not to weaken.

"What?" He looked confused. "What about Rachel?"

"What do you feel for her?"

"How can you ask that?" True fury raced through him that she even had to question his feelings for her daughter. "You know I care about her."

Anne drew a hard breath. "Yes, I do," she admitted truthfully. "I know you care about her." As pain washed over her, she bolted for the door before she changed her mind. "That's not enough."

A second ticked by before her words settled in. "What do you mean?"

"It's not enough," she shouted, needing to match his anger or she'd forget the one promise she'd made to herself for Rachel's sake. At the door, she snatched up the small grocery bag. "It's not enough, Pete."

Chapter Thirteen

Acting like a weepy female never was Anne's style, but during private moments the next morning, she seesawed between crying jags and anger, mainly at herself. She wondered if she would ever forget the hurt she'd seen in Pete's eyes. Or the love she felt for him.

Maybe he'd never understand that for her love wasn't enough. She couldn't let dreams of a life with him overpower the promise she'd made to her daughter.

She finished a cup of coffee, then reached into the grocery bag she'd left on the counter last night. Instead of the formula for Rachel's breakfast, her hand closed over something soft and cuddly.

Anne sagged against the counter. Oh, God. She clutched the teddy bear tightly in her hands, her heart suddenly lurching with misgivings. What if she'd made a mistake?

Pete plunged into work at the office, but he was only going through the motions. All day he'd battled anger, frustration, hurt. Over and over, he wondered why he'd gone through life and had never said those words to any woman but the one who didn't want to hear them. Slamming a desk drawer, he looked up in response to the squeak of his door opening.

"Am I coming at a bad time?"

A touch self-consciously, Pete offered Klein a slim smile and pushed back his chair to stand.

Klein waved him down and closed the door behind him.

Pete didn't need mind-reading ability. A decision must have been made about the partnership. Odd, but it didn't carry the importance for him that it had weeks ago. Nothing mattered but Anne. In retrospect, he wondered what the hell had gone wrong. Had he pushed her too hard? Had he expected too much too soon?

"Peter?"

Pete brought himself back to Klein sitting in a chair across the desk from him.

"I hope you're pleased."

What was it that should please him?

"We'll make the official announcement tomorrow." He went on, "A small celebration with champagne. So everyone can congratulate you properly."

So he'd gotten the partnership. Why didn't he feel satisfaction? Why wasn't he feeling anything?

"Welcome to the firm," he said, offering his hand. "We're all happy to have you as a new partner."

Pete did what was expected, accepting his hand.

Klein smiled. "I can see you're surprised. You shouldn't be. You're the most qualified."

Pete managed a timely smile.

"It really became a very easy decision for us." Klein's thick, white brows bunched as he frowned. "I'd rather not go into details, but Reed and I thought Martin wouldn't fit into our overall policies."

Pete knew the details, just as everyone else around the law firm knew. Cassie had already begun divorce proceedings.

"And Frank..." He looked more troubled. "I've always believed a man should have definite priorities. The firm should be important to him, but if a man's personal life isn't successful, then he'll hardly give his best effort here."

Pete couldn't understand what Klein was talking about.

"His wife had a boy. Did you hear?"

Pete shook his head. "No, I didn't."

He heaved heavily. "You're a partner now. I don't need to withhold anything from you anymore, do I? We learned he chose not to be with her. That disturbed me. The firm's fine reputation has always been based on certain procedures that extend beyond our professional functions. I realize that some of them seem old-fashioned, but those policies have made us the choice of some of the most respected families in society. If his family doesn't come first under those circumstances, how would he ever convey the right qualities to our clients?''

Pete remained quiet, sensing Klein found the topic discomforting.

"No, we couldn't accept that," he said a touch piously. "My wife claims I'm a 'rather nice old geezer.'" He chuckled at himself. "And a touch staid."

Coupled with respect, Pete felt a genuine liking for the man he'd never seen before. "I don't think so."

"Thank you for that. But I seem to have passé notions for this modern world. I believe families are important. That children are the stepping stones to the future."

Somewhat nervously, Anne opened the door of her home to Jerome that evening. Having fought a melancholy mood all day, when he'd called asking if he could stop by to see Rachel, she'd almost welcomed the distraction.

Hesitantly he entered her home. Anne noted the strain in his face of a sleepless night. "Thank you for letting me come." His gaze fell on Rachel, gleefully kicking her legs in the carrier seat.

"I always wanted Rachel to know her grandfather."

He offered a sad, wry smile, but his eyes never left Rachel. "Can I . . ."

Anne guessed his request. A step ahead of him, she lifted Rachel and set her in Jerome's arms.

She fussed for a second then inquisitiveness took over. Eyes wide, she explored with tiny fingers the unfamiliar face of her grandfather.

"I thought when Keith married that he'd settle down," he said, bouncing Rachel on his knee. As if unable to meet Anne's stare, his eyes remained on Rachel as he spoke. "Marriage is just a slip of paper. People don't change because of it. They either are dependable or they're not. He wasn't." He gave his head a shake. "I'm sorry. I'm truly sorry."

He seemed so uncertain that Anne almost wished for a touch of the autocratic manner she was accustomed to. Silent, she left him to visit with Rachel alone and poured coffee before rejoining them.

"What are your plans now, Anne?" he asked as she set a cup on the end table beside him.

"Plans?"

"He's asked you to marry him, hasn't he? I assumed he would," he went on, not waiting for Anne's answer. "And he'll be good to our Rachel."

Stunned, Anne stared at him with the realization that he'd already accepted another man as Rachel's father.

A hint of a smile curved the edges of his lips. "I wouldn't say that if I hadn't seen the fury in his eyes last night. He looked like a man who'd do whatever he had to to prevent me from taking Rachel from you. He's a man who deserves respect. There are few men I feel that way about, but when I tried a power play on him, I failed."

Baffled, Anne laced her hands together. "I don't understand."

Head bent, he studied Rachel. She was just as fascinated with him. "He didn't flinch when I threatened to take away everything he'd worked for."

"Jerome, what are you talking about?" Anne asked with a thread of impatience. "What do you mean? When did you threaten him?"

"When I went to his office." A smile for Rachel remained on his face. "Didn't he tell you?"

As he explained, Anne recalled that Pete had only said Jerome was looking for an ally.

Anne couldn't speak. Pete had promised he wouldn't let Jerome have Rachel and he'd meant it. He'd been willing to give up everything for her and Rachel. How could she not have seen the truth? The answer was simple. She'd been blinded by memories of other men who'd never cared.

"I'm sorry about everything that's happened, Anne," he said with some remorse. "I only wanted Rachel because I did truly believe you would be wrong for her."

Anne focused on him. "I understand," she said softly.

In a manner of disbelief, he shook his head. "I'm grateful you do. I doubt I would be so forgiving. And I know I'm asking a great deal of you. But could we put the past behind us?"

More than anything, she wanted that with him. She edged forward on her chair and touched his arm. "It's time." Yes, it was time, she repeated to herself. Agonizingly she realized how long she'd allowed the past to control her. The end of her marriage to Keith had dredged up a childhood filled with her mother's failures. In the end, she wasn't the fighter she thought she was. She'd given up dreaming, afraid she'd be left as easily now as then.

Stupidly she'd blinded herself, or she'd have seen that Pete had meant the promise he'd made to her. Even if he had to jeopardize his position at the law firm, he'd been willing to battle Jerome to keep Rachel with her.

Ironically he'd become her anchor. They'd agreed to no involvement, yet he'd shouldered responsibility to keep Jerome away from Rachel. They'd agreed to no promises, yet he'd offered her constant assurances. They'd agreed to no commitment, yet he'd pledged to battle alongside her.

Too frightened, she mused. She'd been too frightened or she'd have seen that she had what she'd been looking for all her life—someone she could depend on, someone who wouldn't abandon her. She squeezed her eyes tight in anguish, pain gnawing at her. In her efforts not to be hurt, she'd hurt him. She'd abandoned him.

The house echoed with a silence that was thundering. Unlocking the door that evening, Pete wasn't prepared for the emptiness.

Years of hard work had paid off. He should be celebrating. This was one of the most important days in his life, and he was alone. Who cared but him that he'd become the youngest partner at the firm?

He wandered into the kitchen, the house carrying a hollowness of his lone footsteps. The hurting shadowed him. Baby jars and bottles still lined the top shelf of his refrigerator. Stacks of folded diapers crowded the top of the washing machine in the laundry room, the scent of baby lotion hung in the air.

All his life, he'd kept himself isolated emotionally. He'd seen his father endure too much for the sake of marriage and love. He hadn't understood the heartache, the loneliness he'd suffered—until now.

Pete stared out the window at the snow fluttering by. He'd finally found someone who'd meant everything to him. No, he'd found two beautiful females. And they were gone from his life as quickly as they'd come into it.

Maybe he deserved this, he reflected as his eyes fell on the invitation from his brother. Hadn't he shut out his brothers, hadn't he done to them what their father had done years ago? He'd convinced himself that he didn't want his brothers' problems anymore, but he couldn't recall the last time either of them had called him with one. God, why had he shunned them? Why had he made such a damn mess of everything?

For a long moment, he stared at the telephone before he gathered the guts he'd lacked for too long and punched out David's phone number.

David answered with a cheery hello as if all was right with the world.

"It's Pete. I'm sorry I didn't get back to you sooner."

"Hey, that's okay," his brother said with no hesitation. "Are you coming?" The eagerness was undeniable.

"I'm coming," Pete answered.

"That's great. I mean it, Pete. I want you to meet Ellen. And your niece. Shelly's really beautiful."

Pete smiled. "I bet she is."

"We all..." David paused as if uncertain how to explain. "I've always talked so much about you to Ellen that she feels like she knows you."

"I don't imagine it was all good," Pete said, trying to sweep away the strain he heard in his brother's voice.

"All good," he answered.

"Did you have a memory lapse and forget those meals I served you?"

David gave a hoot of a laugh. "Never." He was silent then. Pete could almost feel him reaching out to him. "Pete, we always knew you did the best you could." His voice grew more serious. "Jimmy and I thought you might want to forget."

Yeah, he had. But he'd forgotten some wonderful memories, some terrific people, too. Pete swallowed against the tightening in his throat. "The years, but not you two."

"Yeah, I know, big brother," David said with a nervous laugh. "Don't think Jimmy and I didn't know what you were going through. You were cheated more than we were."

Pete scowled in confusion. "Cheated?"

"You had all the responsibility."

"I didn't mind." The truth in his words rippled over him. He hadn't minded during those years. He'd loved his brothers too much to even consider what he was giving. He'd only known it wasn't enough.

David released a good-natured laugh. "Sometimes I bet you did. But we knew."

"Knew what?"

"That without you, we'd have had no one."

Pete carried those words with him when he set down the receiver. Dropping to a chair, he faced himself honestly. He needed his family. Maybe he'd always needed them and had been afraid to admit how much he loved them.

All these years, he'd stayed clear of marriage—deliberately. He hadn't wanted to face the fact that he was a family man. He knew how much a child touched the heart. If he had no wife, there would be no children, and he'd never have to give too much of himself to anyone ever again.

Pete cursed out loud. That's what Anne didn't trust, he realized. She saw that in him, knew he'd rejected his own brothers. If he could do that to them, why not Rachel? Protective instincts wouldn't be enough. He had to love Rachel. Dammit, he did. But he'd never told Anne.

So what could he do about it? Camp on her doorstep until she believed him? An unreasonable thing to do, but he didn't feel too sensible or too logical. He was in love. Logic played no part in love.

* * *

Anne drove slowly down the final street toward Pete's house, the smell of the onions on the hamburgers permeating the air in her car. Since leaving the freeway, she hadn't pushed the accelerator beyond fifteen miles per hour, yet the car fishtailed constantly before braking in front of his house.

Through a slanting sheet of snowflakes, Anne eyed his door. What if he'd changed his mind? What if she'd hurt him too badly? Like her, he still bore the scars of having someone he'd loved turn his back on him. And she'd done the same thing.

Her steps faltered as she released a long breath. He wasn't the only one with tenacity, she told herself for courage. She'd make him listen.

Before she had time to consider, she climbed the steps to ring the doorbell. She pushed it several times, then turned and hurried down the steps.

Déjà vu was Pete's first thought when the doorbell chimed. It chimed again several times. In no mood for Tim or anyone with a bottle of champagne and a celebration in mind, he ambled slowly before switching on the light. No one was there.

It took a full second, no more, for him to race through the house to the back door. Without looking out, he flung it open.

Pleasure filled him. He wanted to yank her and the baby into his arms. The emptiness of every hour away from her lingered, but he didn't move. The hurt was still fresh inside him, warning him not to jump to conclusions. He couldn't discard the possibility that she'd only come to collect Rachel's playpen and swing.

Nervously Anne shifted her stance as his gaze fixed unrelentingly on her face. He'd looked at her in a similar fashion the first time they'd met. Serious eyes, Anne thought. He had such serious eyes. She felt a cowardly streak taking hold. What if he didn't invite her in? What if he wouldn't forgive her?

For a moment, Pete thought he saw in her eyes what he was longing for. "What are you doing out in this weather?"

The coolness in his voice sliced through her.

"Why didn't you stay home? Are you crazy?"

Anne straightened her backbone. "Which question first?"

"Why are you here?"

"To see you. And . . ." She brought a bag out from behind her back. "To bring you this as a peace offering."

The fast-food restaurant bag in her hand didn't appease him. "We're having a blizzard and you went out for hamburgers?"

As snow flurries waltzed around her, she shivered. "For you," she said. With effort, she smiled as she offered him the bag. What she wanted to do was touch his face, wrap her arms around him.

Frowning, he snatched the bag from her. "Come in. Rachel's probably freezing." The urge to take her from Anne's arms nearly overwhelmed him. If it hadn't been for her, would he have ever realized how much he was missing, how much he needed both of them?

Anne gave herself some reassurance. He sounded wonderfully angry. She was grateful for any emotion at the moment. Shivering, she entered the warmth of his house.

"You're crazy. Do you realize what could have happened to the two of you?"

"We had a terrible craving." Anne breezed past him, setting Rachel in her swing before placing the bag on the kitchen counter. She heard the nervous edge in her own voice. If only he would smile. If only he would take her in his arms.

"For hamburgers?"

Anne paused in digging into the bag. During the drive, she'd rehearsed what to say. Speeches wouldn't work. She labored for a breath then went for the jackpot. "For you," she answered softly.

"For me?"

Anne dared a look back over her shoulder. The anger in his eyes had changed to a softer expression. "I've been really difficult."

He felt a shaft of longing cut through him. "An understatement," he said simply because he couldn't make himself say more.

Anne noted he still looked leery. She couldn't blame him. "I've been afraid. I kept saying I didn't want promises from you when they were what I wanted most. I tried not to trust you when you've never given me a reason not to."

"And?" He took a step closer. Emotion flooded him with longing to feel her in his arms and never know again the emptiness he'd felt during all those hours away from her.

"And?" Anne parroted while she tried to measure his mood.

"What do you feel now?"

His hair tousled, his jaw shadowed by the stubble of an evening beard, she thought he looked wonderful. Whether he rejected her or not, she couldn't stand another second of the strained conversation. Quickly she made the final move to close the distance until only inches separated them. "I was so afraid. I never meant to hurt you. But I was afraid to take a chance that Rachel—"

She made a small sound as he slipped his arms around her. "I don't think of her as only your child."

"Pete—"

He pressed a fingertip to her lips. "Let me finish. She's my child, too, Anne. I love her as if she were my own."

She hadn't thought it possible to love him more, but her heart swelled, promising to burst.

"I didn't realize how much I loved her, too, until I called my brother." His hand moved up her body as if needing the physical closeness. "For years, I've been weighed down by guilt. After watching my father turn his back on us, I never wanted to need anyone so much. So I turned my back on them, just like he did. But I never stopped caring about them or loving them. They're my family. That's what I wouldn't let myself remember. You were right. I need them. I need them as much as I think they need me. And I need you. And Rachel,'' he added softly.

''I love you.'' The words didn't seem sufficient, to tell him how much he meant to her.

He grinned slowly. ''No doubts?''

Hearing a noticeable roughness in his voice, she caressed his cheek. ''No, no doubts.''

The tenderness in her eyes warmed him. ''I didn't plan to give up.''

He kissed her hard as if determined to stamp his mark on her. Then his lips gentled, and Anne felt again all the tenderness and love she'd closed her mind to for too long. With a soft laugh, she tipped her head back. ''We need to celebrate.''

Amusement danced in his eyes. ''Yeah, we do.''

Anne caught the exhilaration in his voice. ''Do we? What happened with the partnership?''

''Got it,'' he said, feeling pride of his accomplishment for the first time since he'd received the news.

Happiness bubbled within her. ''Now you have everything you wanted.''

He held her tighter. ''Don't you know that I had nothing until you walked in the door?''

''Oh, you've a smooth tongue, Counselor,'' she said, drawing his laugh. ''Well, I'm prepared to celebrate. We brought greasy hamburgers and fries and...'' She started to turn away. He wouldn't let go, more interested in the curve of her neck than her idea.

Anne drew back. ''Be serious.''

''I thought I was being serious.''

Laughing, she twisted away and reached into the diaper bag. "I brought the champagne," she said, holding up the bottle. "Now all I have to do is make an honest man of you."

Smiling eyes met hers. "Is that a proposal?"

"You're quick-witted, too." She fell back into the full embrace of his arms again. "Will you marry me?"

His hands touched her back with a pressure that assured her he didn't plan to let go again. "Marriage is a big commitment."

"Someone reminded me it's also just a slip of paper," Anne said, raising her face to him. "I've already made a commitment of the heart. I thought I should make it legal."

He took her face in his hands. "Did you talk to Rachel about this?"

Anne slid her hands up his back. "We had a conference."

"Did you? And what did she say?"

Behind them, gleeful gibberish wafted on the air as if Rachel was offering her own two cents' worth.

Anne laughed and brushed her lips across his. "She said it was about time."

A chuckle came from deep in his throat. "Now you know why I love her."

"I know how lucky she is to have you," she said on a soft sigh. "Me, too."

* * * * *

Take 4 bestselling love stories FREE

Plus get a FREE surprise gift!

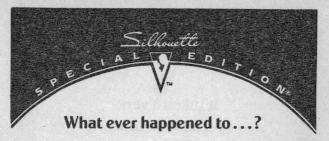

Silhouette

SPECIAL EDITION ®

What ever happened to...?

Have you been wondering when a much-loved character will finally get their own story? Well, have we got a lineup for you! Silhouette Special Edition is proud to present a *Spin-off Spectacular!* Be sure to catch these exciting titles from some of your favorite authors.

TRUE BLUE HEARTS (SE #805 April) *Curtiss Ann Matlock* will have you falling in love with another Breen man. Watch out for Rory!

FALLING FOR RACHEL (SE #810 April) *Those Wild Ukrainians* are back as *Nora Roberts* continues the story of the Stanislaski siblings.

LIVE, LAUGH, LOVE (SE #808 April) *Ada Steward* brings you the lovely story of Jessica, Rebecca's twin from *Hot Wind in Eden* (SE #759).

GRADY'S WEDDING (SE #813 May) In this spin-off to her *Wedding Duet, Patricia McLinn* has bachelor Grady Roberts waiting at the altar.

THE FOREVER NIGHT (SE #816 May) *Myrna Temte*'s popular *Cowboy Country* series is back, and Sheriff Andy Johnson has his own romance!

WHEN SOMEBODY WANTS YOU (SE #822 June) *Trisha Alexander* returns to Louisiana with another tale of love set in the bayou.

KATE'S VOW (SE #823 July) Kate Newton finds her own man to love, honor and cherish in this spin-off of *Sherryl Woods*'s *Vows* series.

WORTH WAITING FOR (SE #825 July) *Bay Matthews* is back and so are some wonderful characters from *Laughter on the Wind* (SE #613).

Don't miss these wonderful titles, only for our readers—only from Silhouette Special Edition!

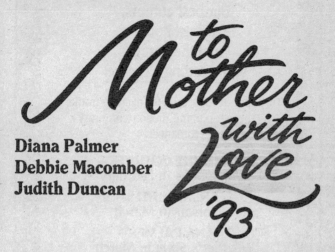 

Silhouette Books
is proud to present
our best authors,
their best books…
and the best in
your reading pleasure!

Throughout 1993, look for exciting books
by these top names in contemporary
romance:

CATHERINE COULTER—
Aftershocks in February

FERN MICHAELS—
Nightstar in March

DIANA PALMER—
Heather's Song in March

ELIZABETH LOWELL
Love Song for a Raven in April

SANDRA BROWN
(previously published under
the pseudonym Erin St. Claire)—
Led Astray in April

LINDA HOWARD—
All That Glitters in May

When it comes to passion,
we wrote the book.

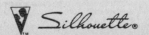

BOBT1RR